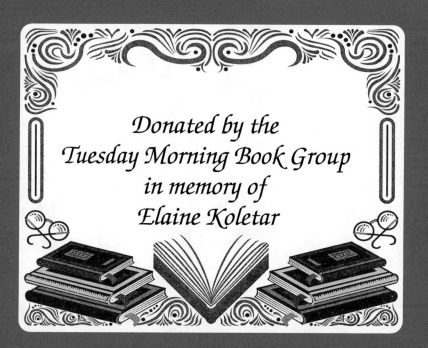

Donated by the
Tuesday Morning Book Group
in memory of
Elaine Koletar

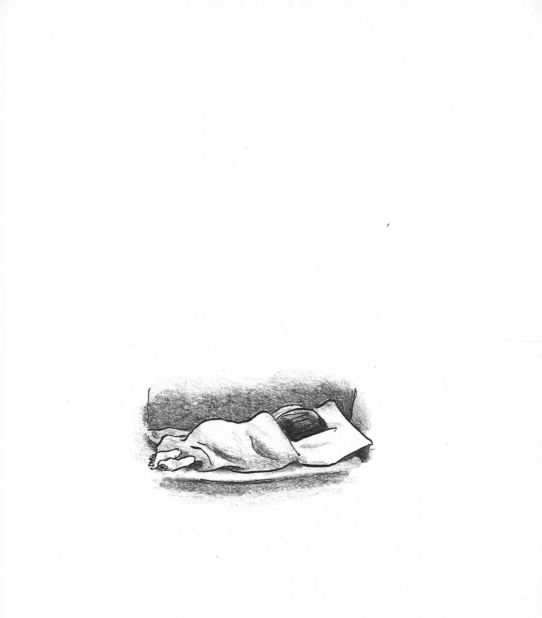

"DON'T FORGET YOUR WHISTLE!" Hope reminded Honey—every morning of every day. Honey *needed* that whistle, in case of emergency, in case things went terribly wrong.

Hope and Honey Scroggins were the closest of sisters, had been right from the start. Truly, they were lucky to love each other so!

Not so lucky when it came to their parents, though.

Mr. and Mrs. Scroggins were simply *awful* people.

THE MEM B

Carolyn COMAN &

ARTHUR A. LEVINE BOOKS

ORY

ANK

Rob SHEPPERSON

AN IMPRINT OF SCHOLASTIC INC.

"FORGET HER."

Hope's father wasn't kidding. He never kidded.

Moments before, he had ordered Honey—Hope's little sister, a skim coat of bubble gum covering most of her small face—out of the car.

"I've told you a thousand times," he said. "No laughing."

Now, as he stepped on the gas and the car lurched back onto the highway, the first words out of his mouth were, "Forget her."

A cyclone of dust rose up in their wake.

Dumbfounded, Hope stared out the rearview window at her sister. For a few seconds she couldn't even make out Honey's little body in the swirl of debris their car wheels had kicked up. By the time she could, Honey had already receded.

"We warned her," Hope's father said.

"Time she learned her lesson," her mother chimed in.

Honey was growing smaller and smaller, her pudgy hand raised in a sad little wave good-bye. Hope opened her mouth to call Honey's name but found she had lost her voice.

"How about meat loaf for dinner?" Hope's father said.

Her mother said, "You and your meat loaf," and reached across the front seat to give his hand a pat.

Hope stared out the window.

Honey was a speck.

Honey was gone!

Oh, gone where?

Hᴏᴘᴇ ʙᴇɢɢᴇᴅ ʜᴇʀ ᴘᴀʀᴇɴᴛs to turn around, to go back.

Onward they sped.

Even after her father had turned off the main road onto another, and then another, and another after that, Hope stared out the back window, searching in vain for her sister.

"Almost home," her mother trilled.

Hope was frantic. "We have to get help . . ."

"No such thing," her father said.

"But Honey . . . !" Hope pleaded.

"Forget her," Mr. Scroggins said. Again.

"That's right," Mrs. Scroggins concurred, and as soon as they got home, her parents threw out Honey's mattress and draped her clothes over low tree branches and scraggly bushes and sold them to passing strangers, along with Honey's toys, for twenty-five cents apiece/five for a dollar.

Hope was left inside with the dust bunnies. Everywhere she turned, everything she saw and didn't see reminded her of Honey, every reminder a jolt to her system.

"Call the police," she begged, when her parents stepped in from the tag sale. "Call *someone.*"

"No phone," her father shrugged, and her mother simply ordered Hope to set the table. "For *three,*" she reminded her.

After dinner, Mr. and Mrs. Scroggins claimed Hope and Honey's bedroom for themselves. Hope had to find another place to sleep.

Dragging her few possessions behind her, Hope continued to plead, "We have to do *something* to get Honey back."

"Honey *who?*" her parents answered in unison, then linked pinky fingers and gave each other a quick peck.

Things didn't get better. Mr. and Mrs. Scroggins referred to Hope as an only child. They followed their own advice and never mentioned Honey again. It was terrible.

One night, as Hope was scrubbing the bathroom floor, a

cry rose up from deep inside her — a cry she could not stifle. "Honey!" she called out.

Mr. Scroggins was in the kitchen making himself a sub, and overheard. "I'm telling you for the *last time*," he warned. "Forget her."

Hope shook her scrub brush up to heaven. She would never forget her, *never*! Honey was lodged deep inside Hope's heart — her broken heart — sheltered there like an egg in its nest.

But the terrible truth that Honey was really and truly gone did take its toll. After a while Hope put on her nightgown, crawled into bed, and simply called it quits.

After Hope called it quits her life took a surprising turn.

Not surprisingly — since she was in bed all the time — she started sleeping a lot more. That was to be expected. What wasn't expected was the windfall, the bombardment, the absolute avalanche of dreams that followed — unlike anything Hope had experienced before. Extreme dreaming opened Hope's eyes to a new and different world. She dreamed her head off! Every night (mornings and afternoons too) she curled up, drifted away, and found behind her eyelids what she couldn't find anywhere else. At least in her dreams, Hope found Honey.

Not that Hope remembered all of her dreams. Or that all of them were happy. Most of them dissolved as soon as she woke up. But they left a residue, a taste — a taste of Honey — and that taste was sweeter by far than anything in her waking life, and made her hungry to dream again, dream more.

Dreaming became the high point of Hope's days and nights. Dreaming gave her something to do, and something to look forward to during the increasingly rare times when she wasn't sleeping. Honestly, awake minutes and hours at the Scroggins residence tended to drag. Occasionally she went into the house to use the bathroom or fix herself a sandwich. She practically never ran into her parents. It was a very long time before they even noticed that Hope had given up and taken to her cot. When it finally did dawn on them, they took all her clothes that weren't pajamas to the consignment store.

One night, between dreams, Hope was sitting all alone at the kitchen table eating a peanut butter sandwich. As she ate, she idly rifled through the mountain of unpaid bills her parents always kept stacked there. What a surprise to discover, among all those sealed envelopes stamped OPEN IMMEDIATELY, a letter addressed to her! Hope could hardly believe her eyes. And despite the fact that she had officially called it quits, her heart raced a bit. No one had ever written her a letter before. This one was thin and official-looking, not unlike the many her parents received just prior to the lights being turned off. But this one definitely had her name on it. And she couldn't stop herself from wondering, from hoping, from believing even for a second that the envelope might contain news of Honey. She set down her sandwich and gave her cheek a little pinch, just to make sure she wasn't already dreaming. She wasn't. Then, with bated breath, she pried the

envelope open with her index finger and pulled out her first letter ever.

Gold letters—WWMB—sat inside a black oval at the top of the page. Hope immediately considered what the letters could stand for: Wobble Wibble Mousy Bites. Weird Weight Mother Babies. Wicked Wasteful Monsters Birthday. She could have gone on guessing for a long time—her mother always said she could waste more time doing nothing than any child ever born—but she was dying to find out what the letter had to say, and so read on:

To: HOPE SCROGGINS

RE: ACCOUNT FLUCTUATION AND/OR IMBALANCE

Hope didn't know what "Re" meant. Or "Fluctuation." And she didn't know what the rest of the letter was talking about either—something about her accounts being in disarray. Something about her bearing full responsibility. Something about *in this time of heightened security*. What did *that* mean, she wondered. It said to refer to case number OXJ38HIl498456JUW09. It said to attend to the matter or face further measures. It said people were standing by to help.

She had trouble imagining that.

The letter was signed by someone named Sterling Prion. What kind of name was *Sterling Prion*, Hope Scroggins asked herself.

She folded the letter and put it back in its envelope. Not a clue, not a whisper, not so much as a *whiff* of news about Honey. Her small shoulders sagged. She didn't even understand the letter. And such an off-putting tone! Overall it left Hope feeling that she'd done something wrong, or might be in trouble. She needed that like a hole in the head.

Oh, she was tired again. Her cot called to her.

Letter and leftovers in hand, Hope made her way back to the garage. She sat on the edge of her cot and finished the last bites of her sandwich. When she was ready to tuck in, she shoved the letter under her bed. She told herself to forget its worrisome warnings and look forward, instead, to whatever dreams awaited her.

Dreams, at least, were free and all she had to do to get them was fall asleep.

A ROARING NOISE CUT SHORT the movie playing inside Hope's head and she startled awake. Everything was dark—it was the middle of the night, after all—but she also was wearing her red satin sleeping mask. She pushed it onto her forehead. Moonlight outlined shapes and shadows around her and Hope saw that the garage door had been opened—that's what had roared into her dream! She sensed she was not alone.

"Honey?" she called out: her first and best hope. And then she saw him—a man—hunched over and wide, standing in the corner among the brooms and shovels.

Springing up on her cot, she asked, "Who are *you*?" It would never have occurred to Hope to call for help, as only her parents were home.

"You Hope Scroggins?"

"Y . . . yeah," she answered.

The barrel-chested man took a step forward. "OK, lezgo," he grunted, then lumbered closer. Suddenly he stopped. "Oh, geez. A kid!" he said. "And look, they got you sleeping in the garage! That's lousy."

Hope had grown used to the garage. She didn't mind it. "Why are you here?" she asked.

"Obleratta and Sons," he answered, perhaps by way of introduction. "Pickup and Delivery."

"Pick up what?"

"You!" he said, but it was really like he was saying, *What else?* He raised his thick hands and twitched his fingers toward himself, indicating she should get a move on. "Lezgo."

"Where?" Hope asked, surprised. She never got to go places. And the notion—of going somewhere, *anywhere*—rose inside her like a bubble.

"WWMB."

WWMB? She remembered those gold initials floating inside their black oval. And just as quickly remembered the letter's vaguely threatening tone.

"Do I have to?" she asked.

"You're on my pickup list," he told her. "They want you."

Now *there* was something Hope had never been told before—that she was wanted. A pleased little grin broke through her effort to stifle it.

"Plus you don't got a choice," Obleratta added, but he didn't rub it in.

Once it was clear how things were going to go, Hope didn't dawdle. She threw some nightgowns—the only clothes she had—into her backpack. She considered leaving her parents a note about where she was going, but quickly realized they wouldn't have the slightest interest. Meanwhile Obleratta was drumming his sausagey fingers on the workbench.

"OK," she said, and then followed him out to his van, which he'd left idling curbside. In the glow of the streetlight she read, emblazoned in green on the van's door: *Obleratta & Sons: Pickup and Delivery Specialists.*

It was the first time since she'd called it quits that Hope had been outside and she felt like the air was kissing her. A lopsided moon hung in the sky. Her parents had never warned her not to leave home in the middle of the night

and ride away with a stranger in a van, and without warning she was finding the experience exhilarating.

"Buckle up," Obleratta said after she'd climbed aboard — another thing no one had ever told her before.

She buckled, and off they went.

As they pulled away Hope turned and looked back at the dilapidated dwelling her parents called home. As far as she was concerned it was only the place where Honey used to be but wasn't anymore. And Hope was more than ready to leave it.

On the road with Obleratta, Hope paid attention to everything. Obleratta, for instance — a man thick in every way: thick neck, thick arms, thick ears even. He was settled into the driver's seat and looked like he *belonged* there. For a while he didn't say anything, just drove. Then he looked over at her and shook his head. He sounded almost apologetic when he said, "When I started in Pickup and Delivery it used to be just things — boxes, buckets. Now they got us moving kids! I dunno. Kids today, you don't got it so easy."

Hope didn't respond. She was actually feeling quite grateful to be leaving her house and going somewhere else. And what was so hard about sitting in a van, in its comfortable seat with plenty of legroom? As far as she was concerned, things were looking up.

Obleratta turned on the radio. "You need anything?" he said.

Hope had never been asked that before. It seemed like a big question and it momentarily stumped her.

"Gum or something. A soda?"

"Oh, sure," she said and he pulled into the mini-mart up the road. Hope had been there once with her parents and Honey—oh! Honey! Hope's heart spasmed at the memory, even as she suddenly worried Obleratta might leave without her.

"Help yourself," he said.

"Huh?"

"Pick something," he told her, pointing to the rack of candy. Obleratta got himself a large coffee to go, then spent a long time loading it with sugar from the glass dispenser. It surprised Hope to see how much sugar could fit. She

studied the rows of candy in front of her and in the end chose Life Savers.

Back in the van, peeling off her first peppermint circle, Hope settled into her seat and asked Obleratta, "What *is* the WWMB, anyway?"

Obleratta repeated each letter, "Dubya, Dubya, Em, Bee," then stuck out his hand like he was hitchhiking and started counting — thumb first: "World." Index finger: "Wide." Middle finger: "Memory." Ring finger: "Bank." He flopped his hand back on the steering wheel and shrugged. "World Wide Memory Bank."

"Oh," Hope said. Her knowledge of banks was limited since her parents rarely earned money and didn't believe in saving any. Then she said, *"Memory* Bank? What memories? Whose?"

"All of 'em." Obleratta shrugged. "Everybody's." He nodded his thick head. "Except for the broken ones — those I take to the Dump."

"Broken memories go to the Dump?" Hope repeated. She was trying to follow.

"Where else?" Obleratta said. "Those deliveries keep me in business."

"That's good," she answered him, not quite sure what they were talking about.

They were quiet for a moment and then Hope asked, "Why do they want *me*?" Even just connecting those two words— *want* and *me*— in the same sentence pleased Hope, and a little smile snuck across her face.

Obleratta shrugged. "I don't ask questions," he said. "I just pick up and deliver."

They drove on, through empty streets and neighborhoods, and Hope tapped out the initials—WWMB—with her fingers. "How far is it?" she asked.

"Right up the road," he answered. "Edge of town."

Hope was sorry to hear their drive wouldn't be lasting longer. She liked chatting with Obleratta, learning about banks for memories, being out in the middle of the night, stopping for coffee and candy. It was the nicest awake time she'd had in ages. She sucked on her Life Saver and looked forward to what they might talk about next.

She couldn't remember the last time she'd had a good conversation.

She didn't have to wait long before Obleratta started in. "My personal opinion?" he said, as if Hope had asked for one. "They should keep kids out of it."

"The Bank?" Hope wondered.

"Nah, their dirty little war."

War? Hope didn't know anything about any war. Of course, her parents didn't follow current events. They considered history a bunch of hooey. Still, shouldn't she have known there was a *war* going on?

Obleratta slurped a sip of coffee. "You got your side that wants to remember, and your side that wants to forget. They're never gonna see eye-to-eye. Why drag kids into it?" He looked over at Hope and nodded. "Am I right?"

Hope nodded back. She didn't really understand what he was talking about but she wanted to hold up her end of the conversation.

"Not that I mind having company, ya know?"

She hoped he meant her.

"S'nice having someone in the passenger seat," he said, and took another glug of coffee.

Once again she smiled.

"Usually it's just me and buckets of cracked memories."

"The ones you take to the Dump?"

Obleratta nodded.

"Where are your sons?" Hope remembered how he had introduced himself, and what it said on the side of the van too: Obleratta & Sons.

He shrugged. "Yeah, well. To tell ya the truth, there aren't any. I just like the idea, ya know? *And Sons*. Got a nice ring to it, dontcha think?"

"Yes," Hope told him. She thought it had a very nice ring to it.

"Plus I always liked that whatchamacallit—ampersand. For the *and*. So I just went ahead and got it painted on. They'll paint whatever you tell 'em to. Hey, a guy can dream, can't he?"

"Oh, *yes*," Hope agreed enthusiastically. She was thrilled to hear they shared an appreciation for dreams, although it came

as news to her that any adults ever dreamed of having children.

Obleratta slowed the van as they approached the last building on the avenue. Lights blazed in the upper story windows. He drove around back and headed down a ramp.

"Here we are," he told her, pulling close to a raised conveyor belt that extended out from the building. He put the van in neutral and turned to her with a shrug and a smile that said their time together, it'd been nice.

Obleratta came around to Hope's side and helped her out of the van. "Lemme give you a hand," he told her, and then lifted Hope under her armpits and set her down on the conveyor belt smooth and steady. Hope thought how good he was at his job—a *specialist*. She remembered the sign on his truck.

Then Obleratta stepped over to the wall and yanked on a big black handle that set the whole thing in motion. Hope began to drift slowly toward the building. "Good luck," he called out. "Here's hopin' it all works out."

"Thanks for everything," she called back as the conveyor

belt carried her forward. She'd enjoyed their ride and was glad to be arriving someplace new. She raised her hand in a friendly wave.

And suddenly, that simple gesture, her own wave good-bye, catapulted Hope back to the memory of another hand — Honey's, waving good-bye in a cyclone of dust — and Hope's heart seized again.

Oh Honey! Where are you?

THE CONVEYOR BELT KEPT ROLLING, with Hope aboard, nearing a section of the wall made up of undulating black strips. Hope braced herself before passing through to the other side and was still standing when she entered the receiving room of the WWMB.

Just a few feet inside the building, the conveyor belt came to a sudden stop and Hope, light as a feather, went flying. (Thinness ran in her family but they also didn't feed her enough.) She landed at the feet of a tall man in a suit.

Hope stepped back and realized he wasn't the only one there. A bunch of grown-ups were positioned around the room, a few uniformed security guards near the conveyor belt, and a number of people behind glass windows on the floor above. All of them were looking down at her, and all of them looked appalled.

The security guards took a step toward her but the man in the suit held up a hand and they stopped. He leaned down a bit and said, ever so politely, "And how may we help you?"

It was such an unexpected question — *help?* Hope remembered her parents laughing at the notion anyone might. Ever. Help. Surely this serious-looking man wasn't serious.

"I'm Hope Scroggins," she blurted.

The tall man knitted his fingers together. "Hmmm." He turned and with a crisp upward nod of his chin dismissed the onlookers. They retreated from their various positions — everyone but the security guards.

Suddenly a woman rushed into the room, a whirling dervish, and called out, "*I'll* handle this, Sterling."

Sterling! The name rang a bell.

"It is a dream matter," the woman declared. Her voice sounded like music. She was dressed in an abundance of layers and colors. When she came closer to introduce herself she nearly enveloped Hope in gauzy material. "Violette Mumm," she cooed. "Guardian of the Dream Vault. Sweet dreams and so nice to meet you. I *love* your nightgown, by the way."

Hope didn't know what to say. She had never received a compliment.

Next, the man identified himself. "Sterling Prion," he said, his voice deep and resonant.

"Please forgive the rather chilly reception," Violette continued. "It's just that we were all expecting . . ." and here she paused.

"An *adult*," Sterling finished. His words sounded like they weighed something.

Violette's face suddenly shone with smile. "So you *surprised* us! Hah! How rare a thing is that in our dreary waking lives! We owe you thanks. Now come with me, I'm *sure* you want to rest," and she draped her long arm with its wingy sleeve across Hope's thin shoulders and guided her toward the staircase.

Hope felt as if she were riding a wave, moving along next to Violette.

Sterling followed, oozing agitation. "Violette, this *isn't* a dream matter. She was summoned because of an account imbalance, because of insufficient *memory* deposits."

Violette pressed on as if he had not spoken.

"Not to mention the matter of security clearance. We can't be ushering outsiders into the Vault at a time when both the Bank and the Dump are under siege from trespass and vandalism!"

Was he talking about the War, Hope wondered? Were they that *close* to it? She found the notion strangely invigorating!

Violette swirled around as if she were the wind itself. "Hope is a *child,* Sterling!" she proclaimed. "Surely that counts for *something* in terms of presumed innocence! And do I need to remind you that she is a *champion* dreamer? We haven't seen dreaming like this in a century! You and your 'account imbalance' are no concern of mine, nor is the reality that some people behave badly in the wide-awake world. The fact remains that Hope Scroggins is a dreamer and she belongs with me! In the Vault!"

Hope's head was spinning. *Champion? Belongs? The Vault?* She had a strong impulse to pinch herself—could she possibly *not* be dreaming?—but she thought twice about making any quick moves. The security guards looked ready to pounce.

Sterling and Violette faced each other in silence for an extended moment and then Sterling acquiesced. "Very well," he said. "Take Miss Scroggins to the Vault and I will conduct the interview there shortly." He even gave Hope a little bow. Hope, clueless but wanting to make a good impression, did the same.

Violette took Hope's hand. And even in the midst of such unfamiliar and confusing circumstances, Hope registered how soft and warm a hand Violette had, and how much she liked holding it. She easily fell into step beside her and followed Violette out of the receiving room and up the stairway. As they neared the top of the stairs, Hope heard what she thought was a waterfall, or a rainstorm on a tin roof—a tremendous rushing sound. And then she stepped into the Hall.

She was stunned by the immensity of the place she'd been delivered to. She would never in a million years have guessed from the outside what the interior held.

She stared, transfixed, at a giant funnel—like a humongous upside-down acorn—suspended from the heavenly ceiling. The noise from it made her teeth buzz. Something—she couldn't see exactly what—was gushing out of the acorn, into the beautiful and intricate structure below. It reminded Hope of a fancy, layered wedding cake. Or maybe the Leaning Tower of Pisa. Hope didn't know *what* it was!

Violette motioned to the vast space before them, and then leaned down close to Hope and said, "Memory Hall. A little full of itself, don't you think?"

Hope thought it was wonderful.

Violette led her down the left side of the Hall. Men in pith helmets, riding bikes with baskets, passed them by. Several tinkled their bells in greeting.

"The Bikers," Violette told Hope. "They deliver to the stacks — the daily memories, run-of-the-mill."

Daily memories, Hope noted. To the stacks — whatever they were.

Violette squeezed Hope's hand and quickened her pace. They zipped past ten-foot-high, foot-thick doors that had huge, brass wheels instead of knobs, as if maybe the rooms behind them could be steered.

Hope could now see just how far back Memory Hall extended, into stacks and stacks of polished, wooden cases — a maze of them — each one dotted with rows of little drawers.

Hope wanted to see more, to take in as much as she could, but Violette pressed ahead quickly to the end of the Hall, to the last door on the left. With grace and ease she turned the brass handle and pushed the massive door open. Then, extending her arm in an elegant gesture of invitation, she told Hope, "Welcome to the place of your dreams!"

Hope looked at Violette. She looked back at Memory Hall. She turned to face the open door. It was a lot to take in. She felt a sudden need to be absolutely sure she wasn't already dreaming. She gave herself an extra firm pinch and then crossed the threshold.

Inside the Dream Vault Hope found herself in yet *another* world — unlike any place she had ever seen before, including Memory Hall! Clearly Violette had decorated it herself, sparing nothing when it came to drapery and shawls and blankets and pillows, every texture and color of fabric, oceans of it. And everywhere — in the center of the room, in nooks and crannies, running up the rounded walls — were places to lie down: beds, bunks, hammocks, cots, couches, tents. A few stationary sleeper cars rested on the train track that ran around the room halfway up to the domed ceiling. Everywhere Hope turned there was a pillowed place to stretch out and rest. She thought of her spot in the garage and for the first time registered that it was rather shabby.

"Put your feet up," Violette urged as soon as she had

closed the door behind them. The noise from Memory Hall completely vanished, replaced by surround-sound lullabies. The lights were dim.

"Mint tea?" Violette rustled over to an elegantly set tray. "A lovely soporific, don't you think?" She brought a china cup and saucer to the settee Hope had chosen.

"How sweet to have a fellow dreamer join me," she said. "Memories tend to get all the attention around here. But *we* know they don't hold a candle to dreams! Speaking of which, you must be dying to . . ." Violette said, lowering the lights another notch. "Surrender, I always say. Give yourself over to sleep. And dreams." She urged Hope to sleep as long and as late as she wanted. "I would never countenance alarms or wake-up calls of any kind," she assured her. Clearly even the thought of them offended her.

Hope, no stranger to the allure of sleep and dreams, lay back and closed her eyes. It had been an odd and eventful night, however, and a barrage of thoughts and questions were bombarding her mind just then. Sleep seemed a distant possibility. She took quick peeks every now and then to make sure she really was where she was—in the Dream Vault of the World Wide Memory Bank (a pleasant memory of Obleratta's fingers counting off the words played back in her mind)—and not home in the garage, or already dreaming. Each time she peeked, she found Violette hovering nearby, graceful as a butterfly. Finally, Hope closed her eyes and began to drift off. The last thing she heard was Violette shushing someone who had entered the chamber.

"Not *now*, Sterling," Violette whispered. "Can't you see we're hard at work?"

Despite all the distractions, Hope did sleep that night— and dream.

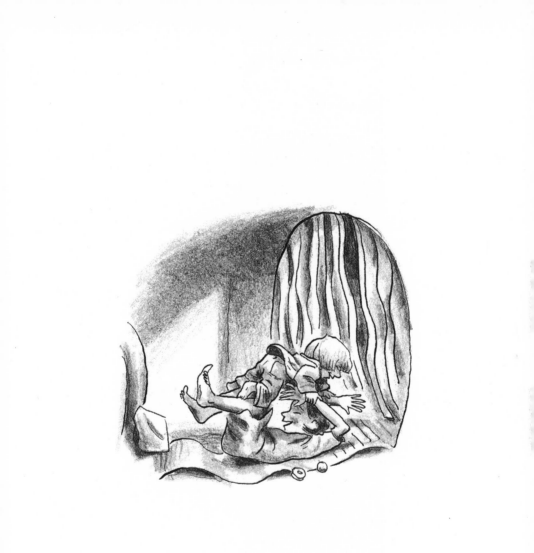

Honey!

Hope sprang up in bed like she was spring-loaded at the waist, her sister's name thundering inside her head. But no sooner had the dream awakened her than it was chased away by what she had awakened to. Where *was* she? Oh yes, yes, now she remembered: the Dream Vault. At the WWMB. And over there Violette, Violette Mumm. It was all coming back to her, and it wasn't a dream. Her pounding heart slowed as her dream galloped off behind her.

Violette was seated at her desk, cinching a small bag with a ribbon.

"Hello," Hope said.

Violette swirled in her seat, "Oh, good morning, my dear. You were *brilliant* again last night. Bravo! Well done!"

Hope was not used to being told she did anything well, much less brilliantly. "I was?" she asked.

"Absolutely. I do believe you're a prodigy."

Hope was not sure, but felt that she had been complimented. "Thank you," she ventured.

"You're amassing a fortune!" Violette told her. "Here, let me get these REMsacks out of the way," and coming over to Hope she began gathering the small leather bags from the settee.

"What are they?"

Violette startled at the question. "Your dreams, naturally!"

"These are my *dreams*?" It was hard to believe. Hope gave herself yet another pinch.

"What *else* would they be?" Violette said. She transferred the last bunch to her desk. "What do you think we store here in the Dream Vault? Dollars and sense?" She tittered at her own small joke.

Her dreams! Hope couldn't get over it—right there in front of her, tied up in little bags!

Violette elegantly raised her arm up to the grand, domed ceiling. "Soon to join all the other dreams ever dreamed, perfect works of art, each and every one."

Hope dropped back her head and stared up, up, up.

She saw, now, that the entire ceiling was embedded with millions of the little sacks. "*All* the dreams?" she said, incredulous.

"Oh yes, my dear," Violette answered. "You can rest assured of that. No dream is lost or overlooked."

"Obleratta didn't tell me you saved *dreams*," Hope told Violette. "He said it was a memory bank."

Violette rolled her eyes. "Memories are the tip of the iceberg. Dreams are the Bank's most valuable asset."

"What about nightmares?" Hope asked.

"Our collection is all-inclusive," Violette answered.

"No Dump?" Hope said. "Like for memories?"

Violette shook her head. "*All* memory is suspect as far as I'm concerned! Some memories imprint more deeply than others, but distortion is inevitable! In any case, we don't make such arbitrary distinctions when it comes to dreams. In our realm, anything goes!" she announced proudly.

"But how do you *get* them?" Hope asked. There were so many things she wanted to know.

Violette's face pinched up a bit. "Oh, the mobile dream

sweepers gather them from outside locations. Here in house we just use the portable collector and monitor." She gestured vaguely toward the contraption at the end of the settee. "I find technology the least interesting part," she said.

But Hope was fascinated. She leaned closer to the gilt-framed screen. It seemed to be pulsing. "Can you *watch* the dreams?" she asked. "Can I watch *mine*?" The sudden possibility of seeing Honey—even on screen—electrified her.

Violette smiled. "I'm afraid not," she said. "We monitor *only* to ensure an impression has been made—never for entertainment, never as voyeurs, never with judgment. The WWMB Honor Code is quite strict."

"Oh," Hope answered, her voice small.

"But *you*, of course, retain as much of your dreams as you remember. And you're free to *tell* your dreams, and find out what they have to tell *you*! I myself *love* a good dream analysis," Violette said, and settled herself on the swooning couch directly opposite Hope. "Go ahead," she urged.

Hope swallowed. She *wanted* to tell her dream—she had never, after all, been asked to tell anyone anything—but she realized that most of the details had already dissolved. All that remained was its essence. "Honey," Hope said, that beautiful name.

Violette nodded appreciatively.

"My sister," she added, even as her heart broke a bit inside her.

"Siblings are fertile dream fodder," Violette said. "Are you close?"

"Oh, yes," Hope answered, "we *are!*" And then, in a knotted voice, burst out, "But she's missing!"

"Missing?" Violette echoed.

"She's gone," Hope said, and her words fell down on her like little rocks. She remembered Honey's little hand waving, and not from any nightmare. "In real life," Hope said.

"Dear!" Violette said. "Oh dear." She reached over and covered Hope's hand with her own. "No *wonder* you've been dreaming so!"

Hope swallowed and tried not to cry.

"Such a dedicated dreamer! You're trying to find your way back to her!"

Hope's eyes got bigger. "I am?" She straightened up. "*Is* there a way? Back to her?" Her heart was galloping in her chest.

"Oh my dear, of that there is no doubt," Violette answered. "And your dreams are leading the way."

"They are?" Hope said, daring to hope.

Oh Honey, there's a way!

"MY TURN, VIOLETTE." Sterling's deep voice echoed inside the chamber.

Hope startled. Her conversation with Violette had set her floating. Now, as she watched Sterling approach — impeccable posture, wrinkle-free — she had the odd sensation that she was coming in for a landing.

"Hello, Miss Scroggins," he said, and offered a slight bow. "I trust you slept well."

She managed only to nod.

"Excellent. Then kindly come with me to discuss your current account activity."

"My account?" Her throat was suddenly dry. Every word he said sounded terribly important, so grown-up.

"Your memory account," he told her, "which, unlike your dream account, has received hardly any recent deposits."

"It hasn't?" she asked in a small voice, sorry even though she wasn't sure for what. Hope looked down at her bags of dreams on the floor — her fortune, Violette had called them, the things that were leading her back to Honey — and realized they didn't count for much with Sterling.

"Come along, then," he said, and ushered Hope out of the Vault. Violette followed close behind.

The roar of Memory Hall greeted them. An endless cascade poured out of the giant funnel in the center of the room.

"The Memory Receptor makes such a *racket,*" Violette said, and covered her ears with her hands.

As much as Hope appreciated the quiet of the Vault, the commotion and energy of the Receptor captivated her too. She craned her neck and squinted her eyes, tried to see exactly what was shooting out its opening. *"Marbles!"* she burst out.

Sterling turned and cast a serious eye on Hope. "The Memory Receptor is receiving incoming *lobeglobes,*" he told her, correction dripping from every word. "Frequently mistaken for marbles, but *not* marbles. *Lobeglobes.* Or as they're commonly called: memories."

Violette swatted in front of her as if a swarm of gnats had appeared.

Hope was seeing *memories*? She stared in amazement at the avalanche of little glass balls gushing out of the Receptor. They sure looked like marbles.

A Biker rode past, tinkled his bell in greeting, and headed off into the maze of wooden stacks directly in front of them. Hope remembered what Violette had told her: They delivered the daily memories. She even remembered that Violette had called them "run-of-the-mill."

Sterling cleared his throat and motioned to the spiral staircase. Looking up, Hope saw an elaborate gated area directly above the Dream Vault.

"Please join me," he said, "in Everlasting Memories."

Hope dutifully began her climb—and if she hadn't been so nervous about the upcoming interview she might have felt she was going to heaven.

At the gate of Everlasting Memories, Sterling turned and made clear his intention to question Hope alone. "You have had your time, Violette. Memory needs to conduct our own investigation and, of course, in private."

Violette's cheeks deepened in color as she turned away.

"Send her back when you're finished," she told Sterling. "She's a dreamer and she *belongs* in the Vault!"

Nervous though she was, Hope loved hearing herself described as belonging. Anywhere.

Sterling opened the gate and Hope stepped inside. The room was, once again, imposingly huge, and she faced a gargantuan wall of shining silver boxes—a million of them, it seemed to Hope, shimmering in the light that poured down from the massive skylight above them. A dazzling sight!

"Welcome to the resting place of everlasting memories," Sterling proclaimed, "the repository of memories that have made the deepest impression, weighty lobeglobes able to withstand the call of forgetting. It is my great privilege to serve as their curator, to oversee the maintenance and protection of the safe deposit boxes you see before you."

"Wow," Hope said, genuinely impressed. The wall of boxes in front of her was as amazing, in its own way, as the Dream Vault's ceiling stuffed with dreams.

"Shall we?" Sterling said, and led her into the giant room.

They walked for a long time, down to a marble-topped

desk. Sterling took a seat behind it, and offered Hope a straight-back chair opposite him. The interview commenced.

"If I recall correctly," Sterling began, "we notified you by mail regarding account irregularity."

"Yes," Hope agreed. The letter. She felt their conversation was off to a good start.

"And when there was no improvement—no increase in deposits to your memory account even as your dream account continued to *soar*—well then, given the current state of affairs, we felt compelled to summon you. Although we had no idea of, well, your condition."

Her *condition*? Hope's eyes opened wider.

"You're a *child*," Sterling stated, clearly sorry that it was so.

"I see," Hope said. Her parents had never thought well of children either.

"Nonetheless, you are here now and there are certain matters that must be straightened out. It's imperative that we investigate every aberration."

It seemed to Hope that she had been called that before: an aberration.

"Especially now, given the growing threat," he said.

"The War?" Hope ventured. She was grateful Obleratta had prepped her.

"Precisely," Sterling said. "With nearly daily incidents of vandalism and trickery occurring, we cannot be too careful. Believe you me, it's no laughing matter," he continued, even though no one was anywhere near laughing. "I'm sure you can understand our position."

Hope was glad he was sure.

"And unfortunately the drastic drop in your memory deposits concurrent with the rapid increase in dreaming fits the profile of CSG meddling. Which cannot and will not be tolerated!"

"No, *sir*!" Hope said.

"So then: What can you tell me about your lack of memory deposits over the last few months? Have your memories been tampered with in any way? Have you been approached by any suspicious characters regarding memory dumping or erasure?"

Before Hope could even begin to answer, Sterling pushed on: "Do you now have, or have you ever had any affiliation whatsoever with the CSG?"

CSG? Hope thought as fast as she could. Cats Sound Good. Candy Sleeps Guilty. Cake Syrup . . .

"*Have* you?" Sterling repeated.

"I . . . I don't think so," she answered. She paused. "What is it?" she asked, her voice a mere squeak. "CSG?"

Sterling's eyes widened. "You've never heard of them?" he said. "The Clean Slate Gang?"

Hope shook her head back and forth.

Sterling nodded up and down. "The CSG," he repeated, grim-faced. "They're a growing army of ruthless, razor-sharp, highly trained saboteurs—their ringleader goes by the name of Tabula Rasa—and they are dedicated to nothing less than the eradication of history! They hold nothing sacred. They mock remembrance of things past, they wreak havoc on the WWMB, they trespass at the Dump. We've received reports of *bonfires*! Explosions of *lobeglobes*!" Sterling twitched even saying so. "I tell you, this rampant disrespect for memory does not bode well. The CSG would just as soon see memories go up in smoke! But the forces of memory must prevail!"

Sterling's pronouncements had a stirring ring to them, but Hope still wasn't clear exactly what they were talking about, or what any of it had to do with her.

"How is it possible you've never heard of the CSG?" he continued. "Do you live in a *cave*?" he asked, in a slight attempt at levity.

"A garage," she told him.

He paused, then gave a little shake of his head. He peered at her and for the first time seemed to see the small child she was, sitting before him in her nightgown.

"Well," he said. "In any case. Now you know. The CSG are a menace and threat to society." He shuddered slightly. "So I must ask: If you have no association with them what-soever, then how do you account for the precipitous drop in your memory deposits? Clearly it's not due to aging." He actually smiled at her then, and Hope saw his clean teeth.

She took a wild stab at an answer: "My parents told me to," she said. "Forget."

Sterling's head angled and he leaned in over his leather blotter. "Told you to forget what?"

"My sister," she said. "Honey." As always, the words panged her.

Sterling's eyebrows shot up. "Your parents told you to forget your sister?" he repeated. "Why?"

"Because *they* had," Hope explained. "But *I* haven't, not a bit," she hastened to add. "I'll *never* forget Honey." She swallowed hard. "All I've been doing lately is sleeping—honest! And dreaming," she added, and saying so, Hope remembered Violette's beautiful assurance that dreams were leading her to Honey.

"I see . . ." Sterling said, tapping his fingers against his cheek. He had picked up a sheet of paper filled with numbers and rows and columns and was studying it. "The daily tally shows that even in the short time since you were picked up and delivered to the Bank your memory deposits have increased. There is still a deficiency, but I do see signs of improvement, and the numbers tend to support your story."

Her *story*? Hope had never thought of her life as a story.

"I'm afraid that we may have been a tad overzealous, Miss Scroggins. Your account appears to be deficient due to natural causes—increased sleeping, decreased involvement in memory-generating real life—and *not*, as we had feared, CSG meddling." He pulled open his desk drawer. "I'll write up my report to that effect and we'll have you back home before you even have time to get homesick."

Hope shuddered. She already *was*: deeply sick of her home. And she had absolutely no desire to return. "Do I have to?" she asked.

"Have to what?"

"Go home?"

"Oh, come now," Sterling said.

"Please let me stay here," Hope begged. She had dreaming to do! She was finding her way to Honey!

"But your parents will be worried . . ."

"About what?" Hope asked.

"Why, *you*, of course!" Sterling answered.

Hope couldn't help it: Her eyes rolled in her head. She remembered Honey waving in the cloud of dust, the discarded mattress, those awful words: "Forget her."

"They've probably already moved," she told him.

Sterling held up his hand. He looked pained. "Miss

Scroggins," he began, "Bank personnel are forbidden from meddling in the personal lives of our depositors. And in any case, parental behavior is not my specialty."

Hope had a brief, fond memory of Obleratta. Now *there* was a specialist!

"But can I stay?" she asked. "Please, please, please?" Her pleading reminded her of how she had begged her parents — to go back, to get Honey! And what good had that done?

Sterling didn't answer and Hope assumed the worst.

Then he cleared his throat and for just a moment his face seemed to soften. "Well," he began. "Given your preference, and the fact your accounts still need to be balanced, I suppose an additional stay — *under certain conditions* — might be in order."

Hope gasped in delight.

"I'll call on Helen, in New Accounts, to help. She seems to like people . . . such as yourself."

"Children." Hope said the word for him.

"Precisely."

"So I get to stay?" Hope's heart soared.

"Provided you continue to progress and barring

catastrophic CSG escalation," Sterling said. "I expect to see your memory account replenished with deposits on a regular basis. Which means you will be up and about, taking things in, gathering the stuff of new memories. Make yourself useful, be of service! No more nonstop sleeping!"

"Oh yes," Hope promised. "I'll serve . . . and remember . . . *and* dream!"

"Very well, then," Sterling said. "I'll call for a Biker to take you to New Accounts. I'd escort you there myself but I have serious business to attend to."

"Oh yes, yes, thank you so much." Hope was skipping backward toward the door.

"And remember," he called out to her, "remain alert and vigilant!"

"You bet!" Hope said. "Alert and vigilant!"

"The CSG!" he railed. "They're out there. And they're dangerous! Given half a chance they'd bury us!"

Remember! The dangerous Clean Slate Gang!

Hope TRIED TO REMAIN VIGILANT about the CSG, but thoughts of them vanished as she sped through Memory Hall on the back of the Biker's gliding bicycle. What a lively, thrumming place it was! She watched as an endless avalanche of marbles—memories—*lobeglobes*, she remembered—poured from the mouth of the grand Receptor. The roar was oceanic.

Women were stationed all around the trough where the lobeglobes rained down, leaning into the deluge, up to their elbows in memories. A few of them waved as Hope whisked by; one raised a swollen thumb in salute and hollered out, "Come visit!" Other Bikers passing by tinkled their bells in greeting. Hope couldn't get over how nice everyone was!

Hope's Biker carried her to the opposite side of Memory Hall, where a squat woman with a soft, white bun at the nape of her neck stood waiting in one of the tall doorways.

"I'm Helen," she introduced herself, and offered Hope a hand down. Then, much to Hope's surprise, she hugged her! "An actual *child* in our midst!" Helen proclaimed, as if that could only be a good thing. The shock of someone being delighted by her presence made Hope's elbows tingle.

Helen ushered Hope into a bright and airy room. "Welcome to New Accounts," she said, "commonly called the Nursery. Here we receive and save the very *first* memories, which are, of course, the start of everything."

She invited Hope to sit down — in a chair that was just her size — and immediately served her chocolate milk. She had also prepared a tray full of little sandwiches with all the crusts cut off. It was Hope's first taste of bread that wasn't stale and she thought it a wondrous thing. She instantly felt at home in the light-drenched Nursery, in a place so completely different from where she used to live. If only Honey were there beside her, eating the crustless sandwiches and giving herself a chocolate milk mustache!

Overhead, birds flitted from perch to perch.

"Would you like a tour?" Helen asked, when all the sandwiches were gone.

Yes, she would! Hope was especially intrigued by the gently whirring contraptions that lined the far wall of the room.

Unlike Violette, Helen was more than happy to talk about equipment. She led Hope to the counter and proudly showed off the highly calibrated distillers. She even used a little pointer to show Hope the individual mechanisms. Helen was a retired pediatric nurse, but she had a bit of schoolteacher in her too. Hope paid close attention, eager to remember everything.

Each receiver operated within a glass dome, quietly humming as it scanned for first memories — which Helen called "memies." They were picked up by ultrasensitive baby monitors, Helen told her, that could detect and transfer first memories over a 1,600-mile radius!

Hope did not know what a radius was, but knew enough to nod appreciatively.

"Once received," Helen told her, "the first memory is bound

with stiffener and then sifted until the merest, sheerest tendrils emerge and flutter down onto the soapstone dish. I've probably seen a million hatch, but each and every time it hits me: Miraculous!"

Just moments later Hope witnessed a hatching with her own eyes, and it *was* miraculous! Something out of nothing! It was a little bit like seeing dawn break, or the start of fog. A vision! For a moment Hope found it hard to believe that such fragile, insubstantial stuff—no more than a snarl of hair, or a puff of dust—could possibly contain a real, first memory.

"All great things start small," Helen reminded her.

And Hope, being small herself, appreciated hearing it.

"'Course, so do *awful* things," Helen added. "My point being that things have to start somewhere. There's always a first—first step, first word, first disappointment. What you're looking at here is a first memory. Welcome to the beginning," she said.

Hope had never thought about there being such things as first memories. Nor had she considered the particular value of something being a "first." Now she thought back to a few of her own: the first time she shoveled the entire driveway by herself; the first time she changed the oil on her parents' car; the first time, just recently, she had received personal correspondence.

"Never underestimate the importance of the beginning," Helen continued. "Of anything. The beginning has the seeds of everything else to come. Where and how something starts out matters!"

Hope wondered, then, what her own very first memory might have been. The gray of the cinderblocks in her bedroom? The sound of her mother's voice telling her to pipe down? Actually, one of her earliest memories—although it couldn't have been her very *first*—was of giving her whistle to Honey, when Honey was just a little baby. The remembrance of it held Hope still for a moment, in its grip.

Beside her, Helen was resetting a receiver. "If you ask me," she continued, "people don't give memies their due. Dreams and later memories—*they* get all the attention around here. Just because memies are young and fresh and small—like children—they tend to get ignored." At that she turned and clutched Hope to her large bosom. "But little ones are the *real* treasures!"

"Treasures," Hope repeated, startled but pleased by the embrace.

Helen released Hope. "Would you like to transfer one?" she asked.

"Oh *yes,*" Hope answered. Yes she would!

Using a long tweezers, Helen showed Hope how to extract from the powdery mass the cotton-candy-like strands of first memory that had just hatched. "Gentle, now," Helen said, as Hope gave it a try. The trick was to lift the memie without jostling it and insert it into a clear plastic globe, like the containers that held prizes in vending machines, Hope remembered—not that her parents had ever let her get one.

She managed the transfer beautifully, and Helen placed the globe inside a felt egg carton. Memies were considered so precious, she told Hope, that they were not subjected to any viewings on the monitors. To avoid excessive

handling they were simply transferred and preserved as received. Helen motioned to the flat file drawers that ringed the entire room. "Labeled and stored with love," Helen told her.

"But how do you know whose memie it *is*?" Hope asked.

"Oh my, memies are *plastered* with identity," Helen told her. "Identity and memies go hand in hand!"

More first memories were hatching inside the glass domes. Overhead, birds hopped from perch to perch. A question suddenly rose up in Hope. "Would my sister's first memory be here?" Her voice wobbled a bit saying the words.

"Naturally!" Helen answered.

"Can I see it?" she asked. "Can I *hold* it?" The thought of holding Honey's first memory in her hands was thrilling to Hope — more intimate, even, than a dream.

"Well I don't see why not," Helen said. She walked over to a large ledger. "What's her name?"

"Honey," Hope whispered. The name had never sounded so sweet, so pure. "Honey Scroggins."

Helen started thumbing through the pages of the large book. "Are you sure?" she said. "I don't see a Scroggins, Honey, listed."

Forgotten again? Hope's heart plummeted. It *had* to be there. "Yes," she said. "Scroggins." And then she stopped. "Sonny!" she announced. Honey's real name was Sonny, due to the fact that her parents had wanted a boy and made no bones about it. It was Hope who had given Honey her nickname.

"Ah," Helen said. "Sonny." She pointed to the stand of filing cabinets in the corner. "Second drawer from the bottom."

Hope skipped across the room, holding her breath. She felt as though she were about to see Honey herself! She reached down and pulled out the drawer.

But it was — quite horribly — empty!

And what happened next was also quite horrible, at least as far as Hope was concerned: She started to cry! She looked down into the empty felt egg carton — no plastic globe, no precious tendrils, no memie at all — and it pulled the rug right out from under her, it felt like losing Honey yet one more time. Despite the fact that she and Honey had been forbidden by both parents to ever, under any circumstances, blubber, Hope couldn't help it. Her chin quivered and her lips trembled and her nose started to run and before she knew it she was crying her eyes out.

Helen was at Hope's side in a flash. She scooped her up and bundled her off to a rocking chair. There she held and rocked her, patted her head. She didn't tell Hope to knock it off or else, she didn't say anything about giving her something to *really* cry about, she didn't even hum "Cry Me a River." She just rocked her, for as long as it took Hope to cry her heart out.

When the great flood was over, Helen went and got a bag of chocolate kisses from her stash in the pantry and she and Hope ate a bunch of them. "Nothing like a good cry," Helen commented, as if Hope had done a fine thing. And when Helen inquired, "What happened?" Hope's whole sad story gushed out of her, uncorked by all her crying. Resting in Helen's deep lap, Hope told Helen about the bubble gum and *no laughing* and leaving Honey behind—the cyclone of dust and her little waving hand and those awful words, "Forget her." She remembered everything, every little detail, and the more she remembered, the more she remembered. "Her whistle!" she said, suddenly, seeing it as clearly in her mind's eye as when she'd handed it to Honey that morning. "I *know* she was wearing it. It's for her to call me—if she needs me." Hope heaved a stuttered sigh.

It was so painful—and at the same time so comforting—to get it all out! When Hope was finally finished, she was exhausted!

"My, my, my," Helen said, "oh *my*." She shook her head back and forth and back and forth.

Hope's head was resting on Helen's chest, and she thought she heard Helen's big heart crack.

"Have some more," Helen said, holding out the bag of kisses.

Hope helped herself. "So I just wanted to see her memie, you know, hold it in my hand," she explained.

"Well of *course*," Helen said.

"But her drawer is *empty*," Hope said, and that memory, fresh as a cut flower, made her lips tremble.

Helen once again shook her head back and forth, but this time she was smiling. "Oh pumpkin," she said, "I should have told you: If a memie isn't in its labeled slot, it's not there for a very special reason! Every once in a very great while a memie arrives of sufficient weight and heat and density that it is immediately transferred to a safe deposit box. Honey's memie must have been sent straight upstairs, to Sterling. Honey's memie isn't missing," Helen reassured Hope. "It's everlasting!"

"Really?" Hope said. She nearly cried all over again, knowing Honey's memory was safe and sound, not disappeared, or forgotten, or lost in a cyclone of dust. It was there, in the Bank—she pictured the vast wall of safe deposit boxes in Everlasting Memories, all of them polished and glowing.

Helen stroked Hope's head and patted her hand. They both ate more chocolate. They finished the bag.

The room grew dim, and then dimmer. Looking up,

they saw what appeared to be a blackened sun outside the Nursery windows.

"I do believe it's an eclipse," Helen marveled. "Now *that's* a first! Oh, such a memorable day in the Nursery!"

It *was* a memorable day, Hope realized, as she rested happily in Helen's lap.

Oh Honey, I hope you're happy too!

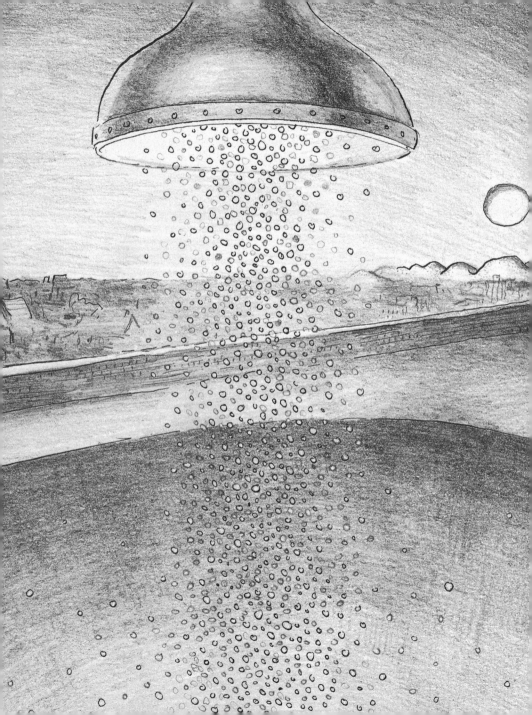

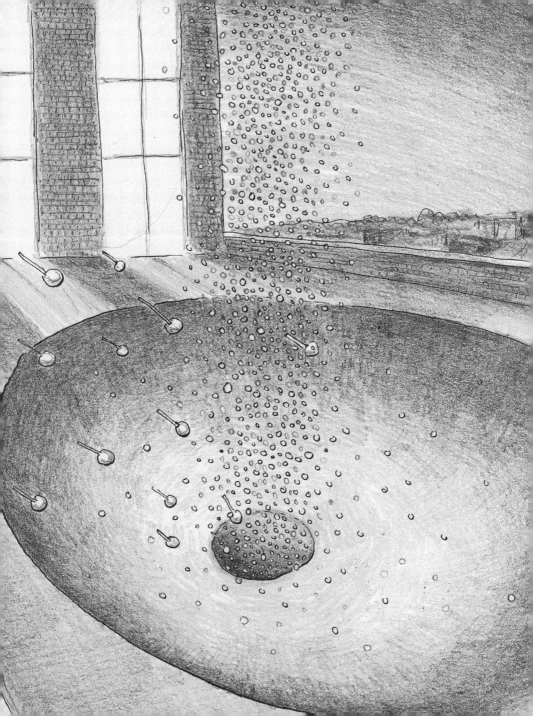

HOPE SAVORED THE LINGERING TASTE of choco-
late as she waited for the Biker Helen had summoned to escort
her back to Memory Hall.

"Come again, come often," Helen told her as they hugged
good-bye. "There will *always* be a place for you here in the
Nursery."

Hope held on to those beautiful words, that promise,
as she and the Biker glided off. Just a little ways into the
stacks they stopped to make a delivery. Hope held his
bike while the Biker unloaded lobeglobes, contained in
small wooden canisters, from his basket. He slotted the
daily memories into one smooth-sliding drawer after
another, and then they were off again, wending their way out
of the stacks and toward the Receptor. When one of the
women workers held up a lobeglobe she'd fished from
the trough and waved it overhead, Hope's Biker responded
immediately.

"For upstairs," she said, handing him a large marble-like

lobeglobe. "Is big one. May be everlasting." Then the woman flashed a tooth-gapped smile at Hope. "You stay with Sorters, angel girl."

Had Hope just been called an *angel*? She beamed.

"I am Ute," the woman bellowed, and pointing to her nearest coworker at the trough, "Is Franka." Ute motioned for Hope to take a seat on the stool between them.

With thanks to the Biker for the ride, Hope climbed from the basket onto the stool. The Biker pedaled off to the dumbwaiter on the far side of Memory Hall.

"Sending lobeglobe upstairs to Sterling man," Ute explained, pointing to the gates of Everlasting Memories. Then she pulled her stocky body up straight, like a soldier, and wiped the smile off her face. "Is serious business," she declared, before she and Franka cackled and went back to their sorting.

On her stool, Hope had a ringside seat for watching the cascade of lobeglobes pour from the funnel, filter down through the columns and tubes, and shoot into the trough. She was amazed by just how many memories there were—how *much* people remembered! Suddenly it struck Hope that *her* memories were part of the never-ending flow too—along with everyone else's in the world! Along with *Honey's*! Oh, how that thought pleased and panged her at the same time! What was Honey remembering, she wondered, and were her memories mixing with Hope's right now, right before her eyes?

With a quick snap of her dimpled wrist, Ute lobbed a lobeglobe from the trough into the bucket at her feet, and it startled Hope.

"For the Dump," Ute hollered.

Hope had a pleasant memory of Obleratta, then, in his van. She imagined him picking up the buckets, delivering them just where they needed to go. She now noticed that all the Sorters occasionally pulled a lobeglobe from the trough and tossed it in the buckets at their feet. They never missed.

"What's wrong with the lobeglobes?" Hope called to Ute.

Withdrawing her hand from the sea of memories, Ute made a little circle with her stubby thumb and index finger. "Is not perfect round," she said. "Not all there." Then

she rotated her pointer finger by her temple. "Is tiny broken," she said.

"But how can you tell?" Hope had to shout for her question to be heard.

Franka hollered back, "These fingers feel *everyting*." She held up her mangled mitts for emphasis. "Nu-ting gets by Franka. *Nu-ting*."

"Do you know whose they *are*?" Hope called out. Maybe they could feel which ones were Honey's!

Franka snatched a lobeglobe out of the trough and closed her swollen digits around it. Within seconds she was dancing a partnerless tango along the perimeter of the Memory Receptor. She was surprisingly light on her feet.

As she passed by Hope she shouted in her ear, "I am holding memory belonging to world's greatest tango dancer. Dark and very handsome man."

Ute slapped her coworker's bottom as she tangoed by, transported.

"Is she kidding?" Hope wanted to know.

Ute just laughed. "Franka can dream. Like rest of us."

As she danced her way back to her place at the Receptor, Franka asked Hope, "You want to try your little fingers?"

In the avalanche of memories? Oh yes, Hope certainly did!

Franka hoisted Hope to the edge of the Receptor and Hope plunged her hands into the sea of incoming lobeglobes. The force and weight of them were shocking. No wonder the Sorters had knuckles the size of Ping-Pong balls! Hope's fingers throbbed after just a few minutes in the trough. As beautiful and fragile as the lobeglobes appeared one by one—exquisite marbles—all together they were a force to be reckoned with!

Hope concentrated on feeling for Honey's memories, but mostly she just got pounded. It amazed her that the Sorters could feel any differences among the lobeglobes—which ones were perfect and which were broken, which were run-of-the-mill and which should be sent upstairs or bucketed for the Dump? Hope kept her hands submerged and tried her hardest, but honestly, they all felt the same to her, all round and smooth.

And sticky! Some of them *definitely* felt sticky! Hope closed her fingers around one and pulled it out—attached to a stick. Not a lobeglobe at all. A lollipop! A red one.

"Uh-oh," Ute hollered. "Is monkey business."

Other Sorters were unearthing lollipops and suckers too—all sizes and shapes and colors—and holding them up.

And just then the alarm blasted.

The sound of it—shrill enough to be heard over the roar of the Receptor—jolted Hope, shot through her like a little bolt of lightning. She pictured Honey in the cyclone, remembered a different whistle altogether.

"Don't be scared, little precious girl," Ute hollered, and she pulled Hope back from the trough. "Is only alarm. Foreign objects make trouble! Guys fix!" She pointed over to Everlasting Memories, where Hope could see Sterling rapidly descending the steps. He approached the Receptor at a fast clip.

"Big deal now," Ute chuckled. "No laughing matter."

Sterling did indeed look grim. He was pulling on a pair of thin white gloves, demanding to see the offending objects, telling the Sorters to stand back and remain calm.

The alarm, mercifully, stopped blaring.

Hope held up the lollipop—red—she'd plucked from the lobeglobes. Sterling went from Sorter to Sorter, pinching each sucker between two latex-covered fingers and then placing it inside a plastic bag.

"All the earmarks of CSG, " he repeated again and again.

Toothmarks too, Hope thought. The lollipop she held was half eaten.

When he reached Hope he seemed surprised to see her, as if he had forgotten she'd ever come to the Bank. He leaned down to take her offering, and told her, darkly, "The enemy is advancing. This is not the place for you to be."

Hope froze. Of *course* it was the place for her to be—surrounded by Honey's memories, dreaming of Honey in the Vault!

Sterling didn't press his point. Instead, he addressed them all. "The Receptor will be searched and cleared of foreign objects," he announced. "In the meantime, please report to the Lounge."

Franka let out a whoop. "Coffee cake!"

"At the sound of the whistle you'll know it's safe to return," Sterling said.

The clanging alarm, even though it had been shut off, was still reverberating inside Hope's head, along with Sterling's worrisome words. Just as she was wondering what to do, where to go, Ute, with one stubby hand against her hip and her elbow out, made a triangle and linked Hope's arm through it. "Stick with Sorters, mine apple dumpling. Will be fine."

Oh, will *everything be fine?*

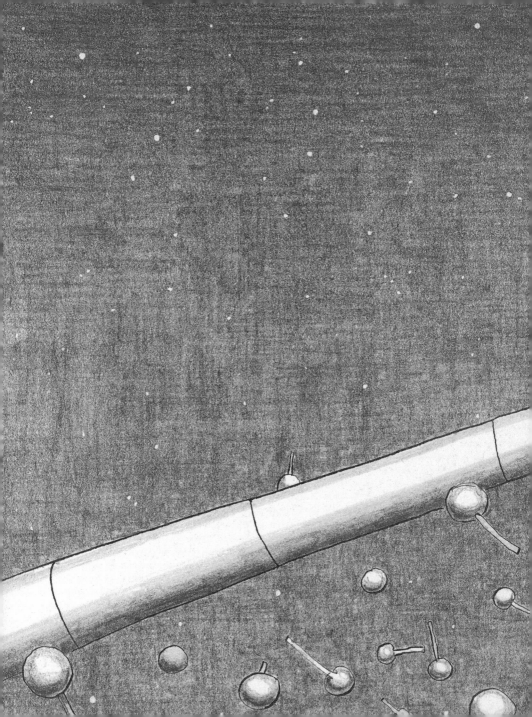

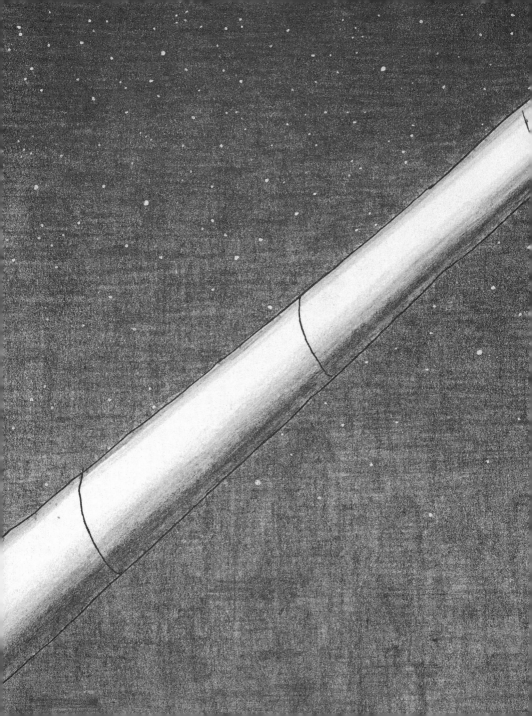

Up IN THE LOUNGE, no one seemed the slightest bit alarmed. Candy in the Receptor? Foreign objects? The CSG? The Sorters' main concern was making sure that Hope ate.

Ute held up Hope's wrist to show the others and declared sadly, "Like toothpick!" Within minutes they had piled a plate high with little wieners and coffee cake and dumplings. Hope had never been fed so well. And worried though she was by what Sterling had said about her leaving the Bank, sheer deliciousness eventually overwhelmed her.

Once they had served themselves, the Sorters began speculating about Obleratta, placing bets on when he would next collect the lobeglobes destined for the Dump.

"*Oh, oh, oh, Obleratta,*" Franka sang, and shimmied her broad shoulders. The others hooted, spraying one another with flying crumbs.

"Is nice boy," Ute confided to Hope.

The Sorters called her *Sweet Patootie* and *Mine Dumpling,* never *Mush-for-Brains* or *What-was-your-name-again?*

Although she had never been to a party, Hope felt like she was at one in the Sorters' Lounge of the WWMB, listening to them talk and laugh, gobbling down coffee cake.

Whenever Sterling's name came up they all lifted their noses into the air and bowed to one another. "Is *terrible* important," Ute said, and everyone laughed. Teasing about Sterling helped Hope forget what he had said to her at the Receptor. She stood up on her seat, raised her fist in the air, and declared, in perfect imitation of him, "Remain alert and vigilant." Which made Ute laugh so hard she choked on her coffee cake; Franka had to pound her with a few flat-palmed whacks on the back.

The Sorters laughed just as much about Violette, whom they clearly thought was nuts. "So vhat did you dhream, my darlink?" they asked one another, flinging imaginary scarves around their throats, sounding not one bit like Violette. Hope laughed along with them — she couldn't help it — even though she felt a little like a traitor. She loved Violette! But sitting with the Sorters in the Lounge, listening to them joke and laugh was irresistible. She was one of the family.

"Eat more of Mama's coffee cake, Schnitzel," Ute ordered,

and passed Hope another piece, veined with cinnamon, topped with brown sugar.

The Sorters talked a lot about their relatives, all of whom came from a place called the Old Country. Each of the Sorters had more siblings than the next. One had six, another eight. Ute held up both her mangled hands. "Ten," she said, nodding up and down. "Ute has ten sisters." Then she nodded back and forth: "Back home. Not here."

"Not here," Hope repeated, her mouth full.

"Other side world," Ute said, shrugging her big shoulders.

"Other side," Hope agreed.

"Where family is?" Ute asked.

Hope saw, in her mind's eye: Honey. She remembered her standing by their mattress at the old house, dressed and ready to go, wearing the whistle Hope always made sure she took with her. . . .

And then it blew: loud and clear, the Bank whistle announcing that it was safe to return.

Oh Honey, are you safe?

"PARTY OVER," Franka said, and Ute wrapped a wedge of coffee cake in a napkin for Hope to eat later. The three of them followed the rest of the Sorters back into Memory Hall.

Suddenly, out of nowhere, came a speeding, roaring motorcycle unit, zooming and swerving, white lights flashing. Ute and Franka yanked Hope out of the way — just in the nick of time!

"Baby girl!" Franka cried.

"Close call!" Ute hollered and shook her meaty arm at the gone-by vehicle.

"What *was* that?" Hope asked. It had all happened so fast! She could have been run over, mowed down. She could have *died*! And the instant she had that thought Hope realized just how much she wanted to *live*! To find Honey! To eat more coffee cake!

"Retrospectors," Ute said. "Gotta keep out an eye."

"How come they're in such a rush?" Hope asked. Her knees were still shaking.

"FMF," Franka said, nodding deeply into her double chins.

Fake More Facts? Families Might Fracture? Fortunately Mistakes Fly? Hope didn't have a clue.

"Final Moment Flashback," Ute explained.

"Final Moment Flashback?" Hope repeated.

"Retrospectors appear—" Ute started.

"—When end is near," Franka finished. "They are all the time in big hurry to get memories for last-minute deliveries."

Hope's eyes got big. "You mean last minutes . . . of a *life?*"

Ute said, "When is time to kick the bucket, dumpling. Buy the farm."

Hope had to be sure. "You mean when you die?"

"Right before," Franka said, her face round as a plate.

Hope was amazed. She hadn't known, hadn't ever thought about such things before. "Is *that* why you save memories—to give them back at the end?"

Ute shrugged. "Is one good reason," she said.

Hope craned her neck to see where the Retrospectors had zoomed off to, spotted them at the base of the spiral staircase, below EM, unloading their basket of lobeglobes.

"How do they know which ones to get?" she asked.

"Memories heat up at the end," Ute told her. "The boys use their thermodetectors to find the hot ones."

"Hot-cha-cha," Franka sang out. She licked her finger, touched her thigh, and made a little hissing sound.

"Then off they go in the encapsulator," Ute said, and Hope watched as the lobeglobes disappeared into the interior column of the staircase—kind of a reverse Memory Receptor.

"So whoever is . . . about to die . . . is getting their memories back right now?"

"A parting gift," Ute said.

"Everyting works out in end," Franka added. "Is nice."

Hope still felt a little weak in the knees. She had taken in so much—everything from memies to Final Moment Flashbacks, the beginning to the end! She felt filled to the brim with things to think about and remember—and dream about too!

"I should probably be getting back to the Vault," she told her friends.

"I call Biker," Ute said. With two fingers in her mouth she blasted a whistle that nearly lifted Hope off her feet.

"Hey, is ok," Franka assured her. "Is only whistle."

"Yes," Hope said, "is whistle."

The Biker arrived, and Franka and Ute gave her bear hugs and pressed the leftover coffee cake into her hands. They didn't want her going to bed hungry.

"Thank you," Hope told them, "for everything." And then she was zipping off down Memory Hall, anxious to see where her dreams might lead her, knowing there wasn't a moment to waste!

"To the Vault," she called out, more ready than ever for sleep and dreams.

Hope awoke from dreaming she was asleep. Her hand was over her heart, pressing.

Oh yes! The whistle! She sprang up in bed still clutching it to her — the thing that wasn't there. A cluster of REMsacks surrounded her on the bed, but her pocket was empty — no REMsack, no whistle! A broken little sound escaped her lips. She felt as if she'd been robbed.

Violette, at her desk, recording the morning delivery of dreams the Bikers had brought in, turned in alarm.

"Dear?" she said, immediately concerned. Sudden awakenings unsettled Violette. She believed in gentle transitions from dreaming into the wide-awake world. "Take as long as you need to come around," she called to Hope. "In your own time." She motioned for the Bikers to finish and depart — they were clipping REMsacks onto the carousel that transported them up to the domed storage area.

Hope lay back down on her bed — a massive thing, Chinese, hundreds of years old, with a wildly engraved headboard. A plump quilt filled with the down of many geese covered her. In the limbo between dreaming and waking, she plucked sadly at the empty pocket of her nightgown. Above her, millions of stored, pulsing dreams filled the domed ceiling. Some of them glowed right through their leather REMsacks and lit up the space like a spray of sparkling stars. Hope stared at the celestial lightshow and after a while asked, "Violette? Why do some glow?"

Violette was preparing their beverages—tea for herself, and hot chocolate for Hope, served in a mug with handles on both sides. She paused to look up and appreciate their heavenly dome. "All dreams can be a source of light," she told Hope, "but some are especially radiant. They linger and continue to shine with all they have to reveal."

"Do you think they tell the *future*?" Hope asked.

"Oh, *everything* tells the future," Violette answered. "And the past too, for that matter—for anyone with eyes to see, and ears to listen."

Hope hadn't known. She'd thought telling the future was more of a big deal than that. Violette made it sound like the future—and the past—were already there somehow, inside of things. Isn't that what Helen had told her too, about beginnings?

Violette scooped a mound of whipped cream onto the cocoa and brought it to Hope, then plumped her pillow so that Hope could stay at least partially reclining. Finally Violette settled herself on the fuschia settee. "Now, then . . ." she said, and Hope knew what was coming.

"Did you dream?"

"The whistle," Hope proclaimed. "I dreamed about Honey's whistle." The image remained, vivid and fresh as a swipe of wet paint across her brain.

Violette nodded appreciatively.

"It's so she can call me," Hope explained. "When she *needs* me!" She sprang up a little in the bed and spilled hot chocolate down the front of her nightgown. "Do you think she's calling me?" she asked. "Is *that* why I dreamed it?"

Violette smiled, calm. "Anything else?"

But the rest of Hope's dream had already begun to fade. "I can't remember!" she said, so plaintively. The thought that Honey might be calling her made Hope hunger for all the

details of her dream! She wanted to know everything! She looked down at the cluster of REMsacks by her bed. "Why can't I just *watch* it?" she asked suddenly. "On the monitor. It's mine, after all!"

"It is most assuredly yours and yours alone," Violette granted. "But dreams are seen during sleep. That's the natural order of things—and part of what makes them dreams."

Hope sighed. She still wished she could just *watch* it, see it with her own eyes.

"And you have whatever you *remember* of your dream," Violette reminded her. "A gentle encouragement, perhaps, for remembering all you can."

"I thought you said all memories were suspect," Hope replied.

Violette smiled. "Well, they *do* take themselves rather seriously, don't they?" she said. "But memories feed dreams. They work together. Besides, without memories we'd bring nothing of our dreams into the wide-awake world, and what a loss *that* would be! So you see they both deserve a place of honor."

Hope stared down at the REMsacks all around her. One of them, she knew — she believed — was holding her whistle dream. "That's where you put it!" she called out — as an image from her dream suddenly came to her. "We put the whistle in the REMsack for safekeeping." Remembering, her heart swelled with love for Violette.

"And Sterling was there," Hope remembered next. It was all flowing back to her now. She felt Sterling's presence behind her, as in the dream. She leaned a little forward in her bed. "He wanted to take it!" she told Violette. "Like it was *his*, or something."

Violette was listening intently. "And?"

Hope's hand flew to her chest, a small bird, and covered her pocket. "We *kept* Honey's whistle," Hope cried, triumphant. "Safe!"

She had remembered her dream, all of it!

Oh Honey, are you remembering?

HOPE NIBBLED her leftover coffee cake, lost in a daydream.

Violette was plumping pillows when a Biker arrived with a message. "It's from Sterling," Violette said, handing Hope the oversized envelope with her name inscribed across it.

"I was just thinking about him!" Hope said. She'd been remembering their encounter at the Receptor. "What a coincidence."

Violette laughed her musical laugh, fanned her long fingers as if shooing something away. "Coincidence is overrated," she insisted. "All things *converge.*"

Hope slid the letter from its envelope. Written in deep blue ink on cream-colored thick stock stationery, the summons requested Hope's presence in Everlasting Memories at her earliest convenience. Despite its agreeable tone and flowery signature—Sterling actually signed it *Your devoted servant*—Hope was wary. What if he told her she had to leave? She wouldn't! She couldn't! She was finding her way to Honey!

In preparation for her visit, Hope washed her feet and donned (a favorite word of Violette's) her best nightgown. She left the Vault with the imprint of Violette's good-bye kiss still fresh on her forehead and climbed the spiral staircase. To calm herself she kept in mind that every step brought her closer to the place of Honey's everlasting memory.

At the very top she turned and saw Ute and Franka far below, wildly waving at her from the Receptor, their stubby fingers all fanned out. Hope gave them a thumbs-up, then turned to the massive gates, took a deep breath, and stepped inside.

Sterling beckoned her down to his desk. "A lobeglobe was sent up and I'm in the midst of an evaluation," he called to her.

Hope certainly didn't mind waiting. She took her time walking down the long carpet, gazed to her heart's content at the wall of silver boxes.

As she came closer, Sterling raised a deep blue lobeglobe up to the light. "Sufficiently large," he muttered. "But size is not the be-all and end-all. Weight is crucial," he informed Hope, and placed the lobeglobe on a shiny scale on the counter.

Hope, who had always been both small and light, didn't know what to make of that information.

"In other words, we're looking for density," he told her, and she brightened, having often been called dense.

"The *true* test of an everlasting memory is its temperature," he said. "Everlasting memories run warm from the beginning."

"And *really* hot at the end!" she contributed. She remembered her lesson about FMFs.

Sterling stopped fiddling with the thermometer he was holding and observed Hope, pleased. "I'm glad to see you are learning!"

Coming from someone who knew everything, the acknowledgment felt especially sweet to Hope.

Sterling then placed the lobeglobe in a chalice-shaped fixture atop the monitor beside his desk. "The final step before certification as an everlasting memory," he told Hope.

The lobeglobe dropped with a plunk and the screen came to life.

Hope was all eyes! She wanted to see! A real everlasting memory!

Sterling cleared his throat. "Please, Miss Scroggins. Depositors are entitled to their privacy. We monitor simply to ensure there is *something* there."

Reluctantly, Hope averted her gaze.

"Now then," Sterling continued. "I believe congratulations are in order."

"They are?" Hope said. The memory playing out beside her still called to her. On the other hand, she had never been congratulated before.

"Your memory deposits have increased," he told her. "And the replenishment continues."

Hope straightened up in her chair. She liked the sound of that word—*replenishment*—whatever it meant.

"Your dream and memory accounts are coming into balance."

She glowed.

"And since all discrepancies have been cleared up and in light of the increasing CSG threat, it seems best for all concerned that you depart the premises, go . . ."

"Go?" Hope yelped. "Go where?" She *belonged* at the Bank. She was on her way to Honey!

"Miss Scroggins," Sterling said, his narrow face pinching up a bit. "As we've discussed, the Bank is not the place for, well . . ." He made a rolling motion with his hand.

"Children," Hope provided.

"Precisely. We have work to do, *important* work. Preservation is our mission." He turned his gaze to the vast wall of everlasting memories.

"But I can help!" Hope cried. "I can work too. Like a rented mule!" She swung her small self around to face the wall of safe deposit boxes—there were surely a million or more. "I'll polish them," she blurted out. "Every one. I'm a champion scrubber!" (Had she just called herself a *champion*?)

Sterling turned to face Hope. He started to object but Hope objected more. "I'll make them glow," she promised. "Like they've never glowed before." She *couldn't* leave the Bank, *wouldn't* turn her back on Honey! "It would be my *privilege*," she finished, in as serious and grand a tone as she had ever mustered.

Sterling hesitated.

Hope hoped.

And then Sterling let out a sigh. "An added shine to the

boxes would be most welcome . . ." he said. "So many of our maintenance crew have been sacrificed to Security during these perilous times."

Hope jumped off her chair, ready to begin. She'd do anything to secure her stay at the Bank, her path to Honey.

Sterling outfitted her with a tool belt, spray bottle, and soft flannel rubbing rags. She strapped on the belt and walked over to the ladder—a tall and steep ladder on wheels that could move along the entire side of the room—and up she went. She was still aquiver from her close call with Sterling, but oh so determined. She would *not* be expelled from the Memory Bank and Dream Vault!

She started at the very top and worked her way down. How bright her buffing made the boxes, how they gleamed in the moonlight that poured through the skylight. She polished each box until she could see her own face in it, rubbed so hard she created a high-pitched vibration that hummed all through her. She polished herself into a kind of trance—and as she gave a final rub to yet another brass handle, she saw—or thought she saw—*did* she see?—for just an instant—*Honey*! Her joyous face, looking out at Hope!

The vision came and went in a blink and Hope was so startled by it that she nearly fell off the ladder. Holding tight to the rung, she stared openmouthed at the safe deposit box in front of her. Honey's face was gone—it was just another shiny surface again—but the *name tag* on it, Hope suddenly realized, engraved in delicate script, read: *Scroggins, Sonny.*

She breathed on the bit of silver, buffed it even brighter, double-checked to make sure she was seeing what was actually there. Then she gave herself a pinch to make extra sure she wasn't dreaming. She was not! Hope Scroggins stood face-to-face with her sister's everlasting memory safe deposit box!

With a shaking hand she grasped the handle and pulled. Sliding out the drawer, she was suddenly so afraid that it would be empty, just as it had been in the Nursery, that she closed her eyes. An instant image of Honey popped up behind her eyelids—Hope's last memory of seeing her, in the cylone of dust, her little hand waving, the silent whistle.

She opened her eyes and looked down. There, in the whole big box, sat one small, perfectly beautiful lobeglobe: Honey's

sole everlasting memory, resting on velvet. Without a thought, before she even breathed out, Hope reached down and scooped up her sister's memory and held it in her palm. It was warm, throbbing. Not large, but solid. Weighty. She should have known. Sterling had told her.

But how can you ever be prepared for holding in your hand the everlasting memory of the person you love most in the world?

"Miss Scroggins," Sterling called.

Hope startled. Her hand closed tight around the lobeglobe.

"I'm needed in the Receiving Room."

Hope looked down from her ladder-top perch and saw Sterling far below.

"Security alert. Numerous foreign objects on the conveyor belt." His voice was somewhat shrill.

Hope did not answer. Honey's warm memie pulsed in her hand.

"Carry on, and I'll be back."

She nodded, finally managed to respond, "All right." But really, all she could think about just then was what she was holding: Honey's memie, her first and everlasting memory. *The seeds of everything else to come,* Helen had said—Hope remembered.

The gates clanged behind him as Sterling rushed out, and Hope stood alone in the grand space of Everlasting Memories.

As if in a trance, still clutching Honey's memory tight, Hope descended the ladder. Without a plan, without a conscious thought of what she would do next, Hope made her way to the monitor beside Sterling's desk, to its blank screen, its empty receptacle—everything ready to receive.

Would she drop Honey's memie in? *Should* she?

Oh Honey, I'd do anything to see you!

"I WANT MINE HOPE!"

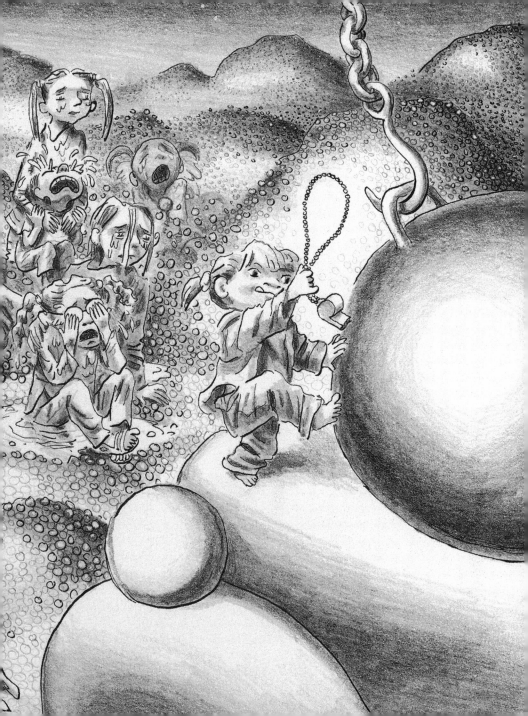

When Honey finally cried out for Hope, *all* the children started remembering things.

"I want my mommy."

"I want my daddy."

"I want my doggie."

"Don't remember and you won't have anything to cry about," Tabby, their leader, exhorted them. "No tears," she commanded—a CSG credo.

But it was too late.

Desperate to stem the remembering, Tabby swung into action. From high above them, she rallied her troops.

"You wanna be a bunch of crybabies?" she taunted them. "Or you wanna be the Clean Slate Gang?"

A few bedraggled children listened up. Honey continued to wail and blow.

"Forget your memories! We've had enough of being dumped on. It's time for us to mess with *their* memories — big time!" Tabby declared. "Follow me," she ordered.

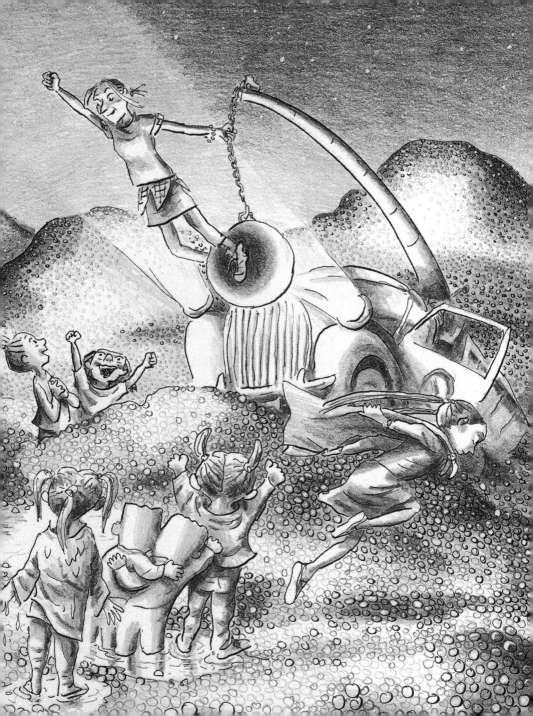

"TO THE BANK!"

"MISS SCROGGINS?" Sterling called out.

Hope whirled at the sound of his voice. Had he *caught* her, seen the memie she was holding? She stood frozen.

Sterling marched down the red carpet and, coming close, towered over Hope. He said nothing.

Hope held her breath.

Finally, he spoke. "Things are heating up."

Honey's memie was hot in her hand. "They are?" Hope squeaked.

He nodded, grim. "Foreign objects galore in Receiving, and reports of yet another disruption at the Dump. A bonfire! Lobeglobes exploding!" He could barely say the words.

"Oh!" Hope exhaled, so enormously relieved it was the CSG and not she who was in trouble. All she could think to say was, "Remain vigilant."

"Indeed," he answered, lost in thought. "Indeed." Finally he focused on Hope. "Clearly I should have evacuated you from the premises earlier. Now I'm afraid it's too late. We may be surrounded."

"Everything will be fine," Hope said. The words just popped out of her mouth. Honey's memie pulsed in her hand.

A slight, sad smile crossed Sterling's face. "Yes, well, let us hope so." He turned toward the wall of everlasting memories. "How did your polishing go?" he asked.

Hope's heart hammered in her chest. She did not want to steal. She did not want to lie. The truth, a bit of it, pushed its way out of her. "Well, I'd been hoping to find Honey's safe deposit box."

Sterling looked perplexed.

"My sister," Hope reminded him.

"Ah, yes. I seem to remember you mentioning something in our initial interview . . ."

"And I'd been wanting to hold her memie . . ." Hope continued.

The corners of Sterling's mouth descended in a sad frown. He shook his head slowly back and forth. "Miss Scroggins," he said. "It's never a good idea to mix personal and professional matters. Polishing is polishing."

"But—" The truth was still trying to push its way out of her, even as Sterling insisted, "Rest assured that your sister's everlasting memory is *exactly* where it needs to be." He raised his arm to the towering wall of safe deposit boxes. "That is where it is, and where it must remain. There can be no exceptions made," he finished.

Hope swallowed. The truth stopped pushing.

"Allow me to personally escort you back to the Vault," he said. "As you might imagine, security is extremely tight."

Hope fell into step behind Sterling. On the descent back down to Memory Hall, Hope heard Ute and Franka calling to her, "Little precious girl!" "Kumquat!" and somehow their cries fortified her. She had not watched it on the monitor, but she would hold Honey's memie in memory of Honey, no matter *what*.

At the Vault door, Sterling reminded Hope, "Alert . . ."

"And vigilant," she responded.

"Just so," Sterling said. "And thank you for services rendered."

"Oh, no," Hope said. "Thank *you*," and opening the door just the thinnest crack, slipped inside like a thief in the night.

Oh Honey! I feel you close to me!

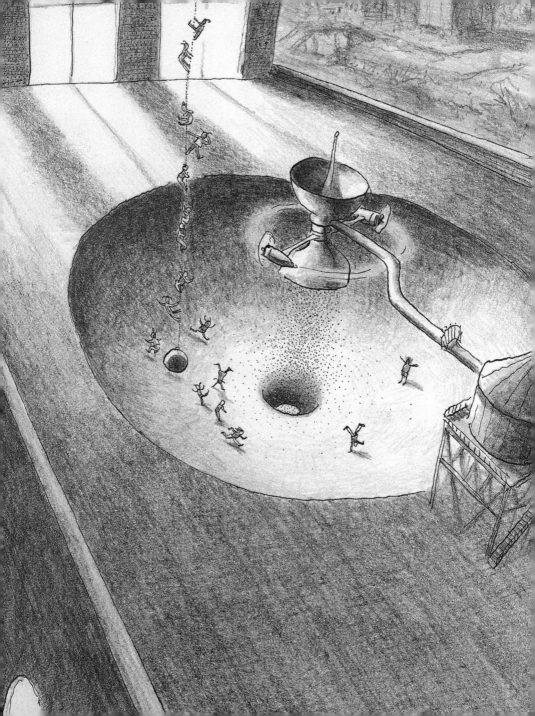

INSIDE THE DIM VAULT all was quiet.

Violette had already retired—on a vermilion-colored chaise lounge, beneath a brocade sheet.

Hope tiptoed to a bed close by and slid underneath the covers, careful not to rustle or thrash. Violette's respect for peace and quiet had made a deep impression on Hope. She stretched out long and straight. Safe at last, she entrusted her treasure—Honey's memie—to the pocket over her heart.

"Good evening," Violette purred.

"Oh!" Hope said. "I thought you were asleep."

"Dozing, dear. Drifting. Delicious."

Hope's hand covered and protected the memory, pressed it against her chest.

"Did your wide-awake hours prove interesting?" Violette asked, her voice like music in the darkened chamber. "The stuff of dreams, perhaps?"

"Oh yes," Hope responded. The vision, finding Honey's

memie, her close call with Sterling at the monitor . . . so much had happened!

"Lovely. And you must be tired," Violette happily suggested.

Hope *was* tired, though her mind still raced. She settled deeper into the bed and tried not to think too much about possible consequences, tried to match her breathing to the pulsing of Honey's memie, warm against her chest. Bit by bit she quieted, and as she did the memory of seeing Honey's face came back to her, silent as smoke.

"I saw her," Hope confided to Violette, almost a whisper. "Looking at me!"

Violette didn't sound the slightest bit surprised. "Aren't moments of expanded vision wonderful?" she said. "So unexpected. So mysterious. Thank *heaven* we have them to punctuate our wide, awake hours. A hedge against boredom, I always say. Déjà vu, for instance."

"Déjà vu?" Hope repeated.

"Some describe it as the experience of parallel memories,

or the intersection of dream and memory. Some call it 'remembering the future'—dreamy developments, all."

Hope lay still, hand over heart. She looked up to the domed ceiling pulsing with saved dreams. A few pouches shone with such intensity, planets among the other twinkling stars. Those must have been some dreams, Hope thought to herself.

"Violette?" she asked.

"Yes?"

"Are you *sure* my dreams are leading me to Honey?"

"Oh, my dear," Violette said, "of course they are—*everything* tends toward reunion. Don't give it a second thought. Don't give it a first thought! Just dream your dreams."

"But do you think I'll *see* Honey again?" Hope pressed.

"Naturally," Violette answered.

"Not only in my dreams," Hope qualified. Dreams were wonderful, she knew, and she looked forward to having many more, but seeing Honey in her dreams wasn't the same as seeing her in the light of day. Hope wanted her real sister. She wanted to give her the biggest hug.

All was quiet in the Vault for a moment, and then Violette spoke. "Most *assuredly* you'll see her in your dreams," she told her. "The rest remains to be seen, and is, I trust, unfolding. Everything will play out."

"Oh," Hope said. Violette's words soothed her, even if she didn't exactly understand all of them. The lobeglobe pulsed against her heart, another source of warmth.

"Not to worry," Violette purred. "Everything is moving forward, my dear."

Hope loved hearing that things were moving forward, toward Honey, and she loved being called *dear*, especially right before she fell asleep and dreamed.

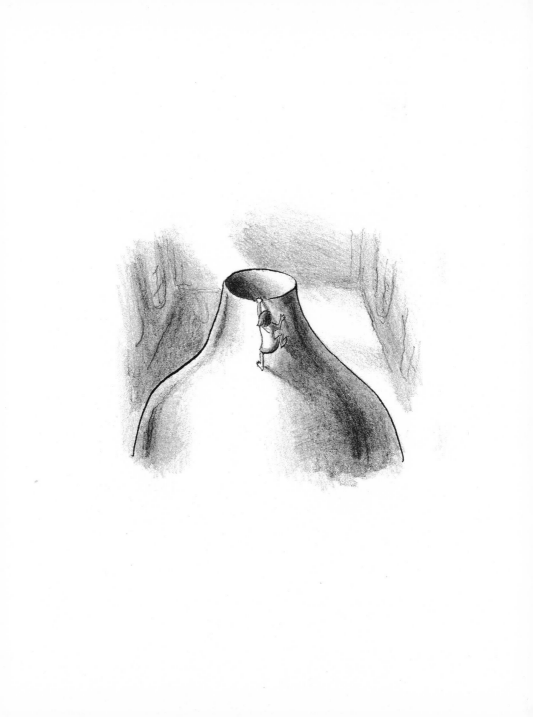

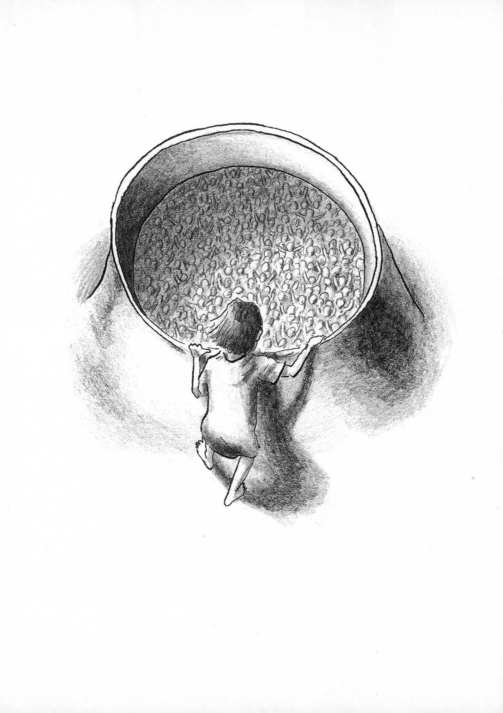

HOPE WOKE WITH A GASP, splattered against her mattress. She was being pounded. Or no, there *was* pounding, but it was on the door. Violette had risen, was whirling around the chamber in a frenzy. "How *dare* they disturb our slumber! This is outrageous."

She pulled open the door; a beam of light shot into the Vault.

"I've come for the stolen memory." Sterling's voice was deeper, more resonant than ever.

Hope sprang up in bed, hand instantly over her heart and Honey's memie.

The door opened wider, the beam of light grew until it included Hope, and Sterling approached.

"No," Hope told him. The word simply escaped her.

"I must insist," he said.

"Sterling," Violette interjected, but he raised his hand as if directing traffic.

"This is beyond your domain. The child has removed an

everlasting memory from its safe deposit box. It must be returned. To where it belongs."

Violette stepped back, out of the shaft of light.

"It belongs with me," Hope said to Sterling. She had learned a thing or two about belonging since arriving at the Bank. Her own voice surprised her—solid and sure.

He extended his hand. "Give it to me now," he said.

It was unthinkable, giving up Honey's memory. She reached in her pocket and pinched the lobeglobe in her fingers, that small warm mass. It was as much of Honey as she had, as close to Honey as she could be.

"I'm warning you," Sterling said—the exact wrong thing to say.

He leaned in to take it and just as he did, Hope pulled back, popped the lobeglobe in her mouth, and swallowed.

Sterling's eyes grew huge. Hope's grew huge too.

"You didn't . . ." Sterling sputtered.

But she had! She could feel it inside her, like a fat, hot pill traveling down her gullet.

Could it *kill* her? she suddenly wondered—but only after she'd already swallowed, and only for a second, because just then an alarm went off in Memory Hall, blasting inside the Dream Vault too. The sound went through Hope like electricity. Was it a *burglar* alarm? And was *she* the burglar?

Sterling rushed off to see what was happening but then caught himself and hurried back. He was not about to surrender the stolen everlasting memory. In one quick move he had Hope securely clamped under his arm, headed toward Memory Hall. He was surprisingly strong for such a brittle man.

Hope had the odd sensation of being a football, raced down the field. As Sterling swept her away she saw Violette holding small pillows over each of her ears to block out the blaring noise.

"Just as I warned," Sterling called to her. "The enemy has attacked!"

Memory Hall was in a state of pandemonium: alarm blaring, everyone running, bikes whizzing by. Sterling raced through the stacks, but finally, winded, he set Hope down.

Her chest was warm, her heart pounding. She and Sterling stared at the Receptor in disbelief.

There were *no* lobeglobes pouring out—not a one! Gone was the roaring sound of rushing memories, and in its place a great grinding noise, over and above the blaring alarm, that pulsed and reverberated throughout Memory Hall. The funnel was blocked, its mouth clogged with something dark and round. Hope felt like she'd seen it all before. Was she dreaming or remembering or was it actually happening? She gave herself a quick pinch with her hot little hand. And then she heard it: *another* sound, on top of or beneath the alarm and the grinding noise, a different sound altogether, something sweet. What was it?

She cocked her head and listened, even as her chest grew warmer and warmer—so warm in fact that she started hopping up and down and fanning herself! In the midst of utter chaos, deafening din, feeling as if she might burst into flames any second, she listened with all her might for the sound she was sure she'd heard.

That's when the Retrospectors arrived — out of nowhere, roaring up on their motorcycles, white lights flashing, sirens blaring. Hope and Sterling spun around and jumped back.

A goggled Retrospector approached, with gizmo raised, beeping, and pointed straight at Hope. She backed away, step after step, but still he kept coming. He was after *her*! Was this the *end*?

"What do you want?" she called out.

"They must be after the everlasting memory you swallowed!" Sterling said.

Hope gasped and clamped both arms across her chest, her hot chest, the burning everlasting memory inside her. But if it was Honey's memory they were after, hot to be claimed, that meant it had to be — but, no, it was too terrible a thought — *Honey's final moment?!*

That's when she heard it again, the sound. And suddenly Hope knew *exactly* what it was: Honey's whistle — pure and clear, coming from the Receptor. Honey was calling! Honey needed her!

Hope tore off running. The Retrospectors followed in hot pursuit, a wild motorcade, Hope kept one step ahead of them all the way to the Receptor. She shot between Ute and Franka, and vaulted over the trough. She scaled one of the interior columns, scrabbling up it like a mountain goat, and climbed to the funnel. She was following the sound of the whistle—the only sound in all the world now—not the alarm, not the grinding of the blockage, just the whistle. Honey's everlasting memory was branding Hope's chest with its intensifying heat even as the sound of the whistle grew faint and fainter.

"I'm coming, Honey," Hope cried out. "Hold on."

She pulled herself to the tip-top of the Receptor and balanced on its edge. The whistle's call—muffled, crushed-sounding—came from just beyond the black ball clogging the mouth of the funnel. Honey was right there, but on the other side!

Hope stretched and reached with everything in her, managed to grab a link of the chain that was dangling from the end of the ball. Then she tugged with all her might, with *more* than all her might.

And it gave! The wrecking ball popped out of the funnel and plummeted into the mouth of the Receptor. Then came the avalanche of backed-up lobeglobes—and buried in its heart, Honey, blowing madly, falling fast.

Hope didn't dawdle. She reached straight into the downpour and pulled her baby sister free.

"I missed you!" Hope cried out, squeezing Honey tight. "Oh, I missed you!"

Honey couldn't *wait* to show Hope her new pigtails.

"You're gonna *love* it here," Hope promised.

"That's where we'll sleep," she told Honey, pointing over to the Dream Vault. "*Best* beds. And Helen, in the Nursery, and chocolate kisses! And those guys over there are Retrospectors." They watched as the tiny goggled men roared away from the Receptor on their motorcycles. No final moment for Honey after all. This was a whole new beginning!

Behind them, the deluge of lobeglobes continued out of the funnel and into the Receptor, a glorious waterfall. Occasionally CSGers exited the funnel along with the lobeglobes, sucked in from the roof and shot into the Receptor, laughing as they went down the tubes.

From high above, Honey waved to her CSG pals down below—the ones who'd been hauled out of the lobeglobes.

After a while Hope noticed how many people down below were looking up. *At them*, it dawned on her, at last. Folks were waving and applauding and calling on Hope and Honey to come down.

"They *want* us!" Hope cried. "They want *us!*"

Honey kicked her little feet in excitement.

"Let's go," Hope said. She swung Honey onto her back, a happy monkey, and nimbly made her way down the side of the Receptor, cheered on by the crowd below.

As soon as they landed, Hope proudly held up Honey for the Sorters to see.

"Sisters!" Ute hollered, and gave a mangled thumbs-up before going back to her rescue work.

Franka danced a cha-cha-cha as she yanked a CSG kid from the deluge.

All around them, chaos reigned, and Hope and Honey watched, delighted.

Suddenly, not far from where they stood, a pair of hands rose up out of the mound of lobeglobes, and grabbed on to the wrecking ball as if for dear life. A moment later a head emerged.

Honey sprang to attention in Hope's arms and waved happily at the new arrival.

The recently rescued children cheered their fearless leader, "Tabby!" A few of them pumped grimy fists into the air and chanted: "C-S-G, C-S-G."

Sterling, sensing danger, summoned Security.

By then the girl had fully emerged from the rubble and was standing tall, feet firmly planted. Hands on hips, she took a good look around her. When she spoke, it was straight to Sterling. "Oh, lighten up, Dad," she said. "We were just fooling around."

"Dad?" Had someone just called Sterling "Dad," Hope wondered.

Sterling's eyebrows and shoulders spiked to the sky.

"Is nice," Ute hollered over. "Have daughter."

"*Martha?* Could that be *you*?"

"That's all in the past. I'm Tabby now."

"It IS you! Mary Martha! What are you doing here? Why aren't you home? Doing your homework?"

"I ran away, Dad. Remember? Like eleven years ago."

"I seem to remember something. . . . Was it really so long ago?"

"Time flies. You've been busy, terribly busy. Everlasting work and all that."

"So . . . does this mean . . . has it really been . . . you *haven't* gone over to the CSG?"

"I *am* the CSG! Tabby, Dad: short for Tabula Rasa. And these are my petite pawns." She motioned to all the kids playing among the lobeglobes. "My army of the lost and abandoned, of which there is no end."

"Honey's not lost!" Hope interjected. "*Or* abandoned!"

Sterling looked apoplectic. "You mean to tell me *you* are responsible for this . . . *chaos*?"

"It *was* my idea," Tabby admitted proudly, and a smile flitted across her face. "Little did we know that Miss Fix-It here would pull the plug and suck us all in for a happy reunion." Tabby glared at Hope, then zoomed in on Honey, sitting contentedly in Hope's arms.

"Come on back," Tabby said, and reached for her.

It was exactly the wrong move.

Honey tightened her thick little arms around Hope and squeezed with all her might.

Up rocketed the lobeglobe Hope had swallowed—hitting Tabby smack in the middle of her forehead—a third eye—and then ricocheting straight into Sterling's chest!

An awkward pause ensued.

"It's an everlasting memory," Sterling said, finally, displaying the marble pinched between his fingers.

"Didn't hurt a bit," Tabby declared, rubbing her head. "Just a lousy little lobeglobe."

"A rare and precious object," Sterling countered, "deserving of preservation and protection."

"Belongs in the Dump," Tabby insisted. "I know a reject when I see one."

Why were they fighting, Hope wondered. What difference did it make? Honey—the one and only real Honey—was right there, safe and sound!

Sterling raised an eyebrow. "I'll be sure to check for damage on the monitor before redepositing it."

Just then, as if on cue, Violette emerged from the Dream Vault, radiantly attired. Behind her was Frank Obleratta, a keg of hot chocolate hoisted on his shoulder.

"Hey, that's the guy who *delivered* me," Hope told Honey. "A specialist."

"You must be *exhausted,*" Violette exhorted each child as she handed out mug after mug of cocoa. "We've been waiting," she whispered to Honey, and added an extra dollop of whipped cream to her cup. Then she welcomed Tabby, her voice like a lullaby: "I know you from your father's dreams." Finally Violette addressed the entire group: "Let us adjourn to the Dream Vault for a slumber party!"

"I must object," Sterling said. "An entire band of, of, of . . ."

"Children!" Violette trilled. "Enough to occupy every bed in the Vault!" Clearly it was a dream come true.

"We cannot simply open our doors to . . ."

"Oh, but we *have*, Sterling, and doors have been opened for *us*. Enough of war. Here we are, young and old, rememberers and forgetters, finally together and on our way to dream. Do please join us!"

"But I have important *work* to do," Sterling resisted. He held up Honey's everlasting memory. "This belongs in its safe deposit box."

"*After* the children are tended," Violette urged. "Children *first*!"

Sterling started to speak, and then stopped. Color rose to his cheeks, and he scanned the crowd for Tabby. Finding her, he offered Violette the slightest bow and then took his place among the masses, right beside his child.

Tabby turned with a wary eye and tried her best to look bored, even as she made room for him beside her. A moment passed and then she asked, "How've you been?"

"Busy," he answered. "You've kept us on our toes."

Tabby smiled. "We try."

"Very well, then," Violette called out. "The Vault awaits."

A cheer rose up, and with Hope and Honey leading the way, the kids took off running.

Hope and Honey stationed themselves at the entrance to the Dream Vault and held open its immense door.

"Welcome to the place of your dreams," Hope called to one and all crossing its threshold.

The CSG kids thundered into the grand room, skittered to find comfy spots, scrambled up ladders to the sleeping cars above, jumped on plump mattresses, dove into tents. They dropped their bedraggled bodies onto cushions of down and lay their heads on plumped pillows.

Tabby watched proudly as her band of ragamuffins claimed places throughout the Vault. Finally, she snagged a hammock for herself and hopped in. Sterling stood close by. After a while, as unobtrusively as possible, he raised his hand and knit his fingers through the webbing. With an almost imperceptible movement, he rocked the hammock, back and forth, back and forth, and his daughter in it.

Hope and Honey waited until all the guests were bedded down and then entered the chamber, letting the massive door close behind them. A grand sleigh bed in the center of the room had been reserved for them—the place of honor—and now they took their rightful place in it.

As they climbed under the covers and snuggled in, a spontaneous burst of applause filled the Vault.

Violette swirled from bed to bed, bestowing good-night kisses, blowing more from her palm up to the children she couldn't reach. She lowered the lights and set the music playing.

Sterling bowed to Violette and tiptoed toward the door.

Throughout the Vault, all grew quiet and still.

Two by two, eyelids closed.

One by one, children surrendered to sleep.

In a perfectly unforgettable moment,
Hope held Honey, Honey held Hope,
and their dreams were sweet.

FOR BELLE

—C.C.

FOR ANNA

AND NINA

—R.S.

ALSO BY
CAROLYN COMAN

MANY STONES

BEE & JACKY

WHAT JAMIE SAW

TELL ME EVERYTHING

LOSING THINGS AT MR. MUDD'S

ALSO BY
CAROLYN COMAN
&
ROB SHEPPERSON

SNEAKING SUSPICIONS

THE BIG HOUSE

Text copyright © 2010 by Carolyn Coman

Illustrations copyright © 2010 by Rob Shepperson

LIBRARY OF CONGRESS CATALOGING-IN-PUBLICATION DATA

Coman, Carolyn.

The Memory Bank / by Carolyn Coman ; illustrations by Rob Shepperson. — 1st ed. p. cm.

Summary: When Hope learns that, while her memory account is seriously low, she is a champion

dreamer, she stays at the World Wide Memory Bank trying to locate her sister Honey, whom their

parents abandoned and told Hope to forget.

ISBN 978-0-545-21066-9 (hardcover : alk. paper) [1. Sisters—Fiction. 2. Memory—Fiction.

3. Dreams—Fiction. 4. Banks and banking—Fiction. 5. Sabotage—Fiction.]

I. Shepperson, Rob, ill. II. Title. PZ7.C729Mem 2010 [Fic]—dc22 2009046851

10 9 8 7 6 5 4 3 2 1   10 11 12 13 14

Printed in the U.S.A.   23

First edition, October 2010

This book was edited by Arthur Levine and Stephen Roxburgh. It was art directed and designed by Marijka Kostiw. The jacket art was created in pen and ink and watercolor. Interior art was created in pen and ink and pencil. The text was set in 13-pt. Adobe Garamond Pro Regular, a typeface based on the type designs of sixteenth-century printer Claude Garamond. Display type was set in Trajan Pro Bold, designed by Carol Twombly in 1989 for Adobe. The design is based on the letterforms of *capitalis monumentalis* or Roman square capitals, as used for the inscription at the base of Trajan's Column, from which the typeface takes its name. The book was printed and bound at R. R. Donnelley in Crawfordsville, Indiana. Production was supervised by Cheryl Weisman, and manufacturing was supervised by Jess White.